Cover Copy

Wishing…for a Highlander

Annie MacLeod needs to choose a husband before the king decides on one for her. Once she arrives at court, she begins searching for a suitable match, except she soon discovers the one man she's always desired is the one man she can never have.

Highland warrior guardian Colin MacLean has long been captivated by Annie. She's the girl he grew up adoring, and the woman who now holds his heart, yet he's at court for a very specific reason. His mission is to free his chief from the king's dungeons, not to taste the sweet temptation of a love that can never be.

When treachery abounds and Annie is kidnapped by Colin's enemy, desire and duty war within him. Can he find a way to rescue the woman he loves…and save the chief he's given his loyalty to?

Books by Joanne Wadsworth

The Matheson Brothers Series
Highlander's Desire, Book One
Highlander's Passion, Book Two
Highlander's Seduction, Book Three
Highlander's Kiss, Book Four
Highlander's Heart, Book Five
Highlander's Sword, Book Six
Highlander's Bride, Book Seven
Highlander's Caress, Book Eight
Highlander's Touch, Book Nine
Highlander's Shifter, Book Ten
Highlander's Claim, Book Eleven
Highlander's Courage, Book Twelve
Highlander's Mermaid, Book Thirteen

Highlander Heat Series
Highlander's Castle, Book One
Highlander's Magic, Book Two
Highlander's Charm, Book Three
Highlander's Guardian, Book Four
Highlander's Faerie, Book Five
Highlander's Champion, Book Six
Highlander's Captive (Short Story)

Billionaire Bodyguards Series
Billionaire Bodyguard Attraction, Book One
Billionaire Bodyguard Boss, Book Two
Billionaire Bodyguard Fling, Book Three

Books by Joanne Wadsworth

Regency Brides Series

The Duke's Bride, Book One

The Earl's Bride, Book Two

The Wartime Bride, Book Three

The Earl's Secret Bride, Book Four

The Prince's Bride, Book Five

Her Pirate Prince, Book Six

Princesses of Myth Series

Protector, Book One

Warrior, Book Two

Hunter (Short Story - Included in Warrior, Book Two)

Enchanter, Book Three

Healer, Book Four

Chaser, Book Five

Highlander's Guardian

Highlander Heat, Book Four

JOANNE WADSWORTH

Dedication

This one is for my wonderful and feisty Nanna who turned ninety this year. Iris Merle Howarth.

Acknowledgements

I have an incredibly supportive family who allow me so much time to write. Huge thanks go to my hubby, Jason, and kiddies, Marisa, Caleb, Cruise and Rocco. Hugs.

For my readers, I can't thank you enough for joining me, and taking this journey to where imagination and magic soar.

Chapter 1

Holyrood House, Edinburgh, 1590.

Tension tightened every muscle in Annie MacLeod's body as she hid behind a tree in the sprawling park near Holyrood House. Clutching the rough bark, she snuck a look around the wide trunk. Twenty feet away, one of her two guardians, Colin MacLean, paced a muddy track between two elm trees, his brow furrowed.

Of all the luck. She'd stumbled upon Colin in this secluded wooded area yesterday after he'd arrived at the king's palace. If he discovered her outside again without an adequate guard or chaperone, she'd be in twice the trouble. Aye, Colin would believe she was up to old tricks, following him as she'd done throughout her childhood.

Hands bunched in her thick burgundy skirts, she crept back a step and crunched on the thick matting of autumn leaves. Drat. Hardly needing to give her location away, she held perfectly still, then carefully, slowly, she slid her other foot back to join the other. No crunching.

Now, one step at a time and she'd escape without notice.

She eased back again, but her slipper sank into soggy soil at the edge of the trail. Precariously close to a thorny bush, she wobbled. When would she ever—

"Annie MacLeod," Colin growled as he came out of nowhere, gripped her waist and hauled her back to safety. "What are you doing in the middle of the forest without a guard, yet again?"

"Ah, I was walking, although apparently no' very well. Thank you for your aid." Her heart pounded and she covered his hands with hers. His fingers, so big and warm, splayed wide over her waist. Colin could move with such stealth and speed. "Please, dinnae tell Rory you've seen me."

"And why should I do that? Where's your aunt?"

"I didnae care to wake her, and Rory's so busy with the king. Interrupting him in order to ask for a guard wasnae something I wished to do."

"Then you should have interrupted me. I'm your guardian, just as Rory is."

"As you can see I did." She smiled, as sweetly as she could in the hope of diverting his attention. "In an indirect sort of way."

"'Tis just as well I heard you, and dinnae give me that sly smile of yours, you scamp."

She smiled wider. Colin may be her guardian, but he was also one of her nearest and dearest. "I couldnae help but notice how worried you looked. Is all well?"

"As well as can be considering my chief is in the cells." He released her and clasped one hand over the hilt of his side sword. The move stretched the fine silk of his black doublet over his broad chest. "Are you aware the MacDonalds of Skye arrived this morn? They remain a distinct threat against your MacLeod and my MacLean kin. You're no' to wander about like this again. If aught happened to you, I'd never forgive myself. Every precaution must be taken."

"The king will never allow the clans to fight while at

court." She touched the frown line slashing his brow and smoothed it out. "I hate to see you worry so."

"That does no' mean they willnae take their quarrels outside, and that is where we are."

"I needed some fresh air and time to think. It isnae easy trying to find a husband amongst the pomp of courtiers who are here." She'd been hounded of late. Like fresh meat to the market, they'd soon learnt she was here at Rory's bidding to choose a husband before the king did so for her, and not for the first time, but the second. Her first contracted handfast had failed, and once was enough. This time Rory had given her the choice to find a suitable match, a rare thing allowed for a woman and an offer she'd pounced on and accepted.

"If you wish aid in finding a husband, I'm here." Colin stroked a finger under her chin, his gaze softening and his touch comforting her. "You need only ask and I'll do whatever I can to help you."

"You're here for your chief and I cannae take you away from that duty." His chief had been captured by the king's men and tossed into Holyrood's tower for his part in the current feud between the clans. She'd been surprised to hear of it. Certainly a great chief like Lachlan MacLean didn't deserve to be treated so.

"I'm here for you as well, and we're kin."

Aye, their grandparents had been cousins, their mothers the closest of friends. On the Isle of Mull, she'd grown up traipsing around after Colin like an adoring child. He'd been so much older and wiser, the gap between them a wide six years, although now she'd turned one and twenty, that divide no longer seemed any great distance at all. "I miss roaming around Mull and being young and carefree. With you."

"Aye, our childhood is gone afore we know it, but since you're still successfully sneaking out after me, you're apparently missing very little." He grinned and her heart lightened at seeing his worry ease.

"I used to don a pair of your old breeches to make my escape less noticeable, but for some reason you always used to sense me nearby regardless." She'd idolized Colin, had missed him and his brother terribly when she'd left at thirteen for the Isle of Skye. Rory MacLeod, her chief and cousin, had requested her father's return to Dunvegan Castle upon Rory's eldest brother's death, and though her mother was a MacLean, her father was a MacLeod and had been honor bound to answer Rory's call-to-arms. Her father had joined Rory as the feud between them and the nearby MacDonald clan had escalated. "Just afore you said the MacDonalds had arrived. Whom exactly?"

"The MacDonald chief's nephews, James and Hugh, as well as a dozen of their warriors."

Not the best news, although not entirely unexpected. The MacDonald chief and his brother both resided in the tower along with Colin's chief. The king had captured each of the three clan chiefs involved in the feud and demanded they enter into talks, albeit behind bars.

"Colin, I know James." As much as she detested the MacDonalds, James was different. James was the younger brother of the man the king had first ordered her to handfast with. In the sennight before she was supposed to speak her vows, she'd stayed at the MacDonald's stronghold and discovered James wished for peace, as greatly as she did. He'd been attentive and kind to her while she'd awaited his brother's return. As luck would have it, his brother had instead fallen in love and wed one of her kin with a close namesake, Anne MacLeod. His subsequent marriage to Anne had nullified their coming handfast and she'd been released to return to her MacLeod kin. "James was naught but kind to me while I stayed at Dunscaith Castle."

"Annie, all MacDonalds are a threat. You must no' become complacent around them."

Aye, anything she said right now in James's defense

wouldn't change Colin's opinion, particularly when she too detested the MacDonald chief. Donald MacDonald was a warrior who wanted it all, and if a clan stood in his way, he battled to remove them. Glad she was she'd never met him. "James is still different to his warmongering uncle, one of the few MacDonalds who is."

"The MacDonalds are all alike. Something you will learn in time." His golden eyes darkened and by his determined expression, his mind was clearly set. "I cannae believe Rory didnae send word to me of the king's handfast demand. That he would tie you to a MacDonald is despicable."

"He had no choice. The king forced his hand." Rory loathed the MacDonalds as much as Colin did, although Rory wished for peace and was willing to negotiate to a certain degree.

"I still should have been told. You're my ward, as much as you are Rory's."

"I asked him no' to tell you." She'd pleaded with Rory that he not send a missive to Colin on Mull. "Colin, your fury would have erupted and caused more problems than what I'd been attempting to solve. I was trying to bring about peace, no' escalate the war."

"The king still forces his wishes upon us. He needs to leave us alone to resolve our own issues, no' alter the way we settle our disputes." His pacing resumed as he tugged at his collar. "Even now, you're still being forced to find a husband when 'tis the last thing you wish."

"At least Rory has afforded me the choice, something I didnae have afore." Which so far had been of little more help. Since she'd arrived at the king's palace and begun her search, she'd been comparing every possible suitor to Colin. She wanted a man like him who would stand by her and her clan's side, caring for each and every one in turn. Even now his concern was etched heavily on his face. "You would make a wonderful husband. Have you ever thought of taking a wife?"

"I war too much."

"Aye, and you also argue too much." She couldn't help the tease.

"Arguing is good for the soul."

"A wife is also good for the soul."

A smile lifted his lips. "I fear, I would only argue with her as well."

"She would need to be rather resilient." She caught his hands, his palms warm against hers and hopping backward, tugged him along the path. "Let's walk afore the day is done. Then you may argue with me some more. I know how much you enjoy that."

"A walk would be good, and watch your step, Annie." He turned her around, slid her hand through his crooked arm and guided her down the trail that led deeper into the woods. "I've missed you and your liveliness."

"I've missed you too." The foliage above thickened, blocking what little remained of the late afternoon sunshine, but Colin's solid presence warmed her through as it always did. "Last month your visit to Dunvegan Castle was so short. We didnae even get to speak."

"I'm sorry about that, scamp." He squeezed her hand, his voice tender as he used her childhood nickname. "I had only a few hours to spare afore I had to return to Duart Castle."

"Is that when your chief was first captured?"

"Aye, and we expected the MacDonalds to attack with their full force upon hearing the news. That was why I came to Dunvegan, to seek Rory's aid and some additional men for the battle, only I discovered from him both the MacDonald of Sleat and the MacDonald of Dunnyveg too had been captured by the king's men. Rory confirmed the two MacDonald clans were in as much turmoil as ours by the loss of their chiefs." He stepped ahead and held up a low branch so she could pass through. "Come, less about my problems when I need to consider yours.

If you wish aid in finding a husband, then allow me to see who's at court this eve and consider any possible prospects."

"Elizabeth has introduced me to almost every unmarried man since I arrived, even Lord Sinclare who must be at least seventy." She rolled her eyes, not impressed at all that she had to consider a man who needed two canes to walk stably with.

"You mean old Batten-face Sinclare is a possible suitor?" He chuckled and she slapped his arm.

"Dinnae laugh. I have no desire to be that man's wife."

"Ah, but consider the benefits. He'd have years of wisdom to offer you."

"Aye, but no' years to give it. When he and I spoke, he made it quite clear he's here to find a young wife in order to provide him with an heir since both his sons passed. I do feel sorry for him, but no' enough to accept a proposal."

"His sons perished in a battle that took many lives. They were good men. I knew them." Colin withdrew his sword and slashed a thorny bush blocking the thin path before stepping through. "We're almost there."

"Almost where?" Birds twittered from their nests above, the forest so thick that nothing but the trees surrounded them.

"On a past trip, I discovered this loch, though 'tis well hidden." Colin returned to her, bent and brushed a soft kiss against her forehead. "Look ahead. I've cleared the way."

He stepped aside and she gasped.

The loch was small, private and completely hidden, its glassy surface dancing with the reflection of the towering trees encircling it. "'Tis beautiful."

"And all ours. How about we have some fun? Like old times."

"You hardly need to ask." His form of fun spoke to her heart and always had. She skipped to the water's edge, lifted her skirts and knelt on the spongy moss. With her hands cupped, she dipped them into the clear water and sipped. "Is this place completely secluded?"

"You wish to swim?"

"You know I do." He'd been able to read her mind for years. She loosened the ties of her burgundy jacket, slipped it off her shoulders and laid it overtop a boulder. "Will you come too?"

"Aye, I can wear my tunic." Turning, he gave her his broad back.

"Thank you for bringing me here. This is exactly what I needed." He'd always been able to ease her worries as none other could. She unlaced her gown's front stays and shed it along with her stockings, leaving her sark as adequate coverage. Then with care, tugged the pins from her hair and swished her head from side to side and released the long golden length. "Do you feel better too?"

"I always do around you, my wee scamp." He divested himself of his weapons, a sword and dirk before shrugging off his doublet. His dark hair wisped with blond ends brushed his shoulders as he bent and hauled off his boots.

She should avert her gaze, but she wasn't nearly as chivalrous as Colin. Instead, as he shucked his leather trews and his white tunic fluttered against him mid-thigh, she smiled with appreciation at the sight of his muscled legs. "Oh, Colin, I'm having the most scandalous thoughts."

"Are you watching me?" He glanced over his shoulder and sighed, rather raggedly. "You're looking for trouble with that kind of expression on your face."

"I'm sorry, but I couldn't help myself. Let's swim." Smiling, she rolled her sark's thin ivory cotton sleeves to the elbow. At the bank's edge, she dove into the pool and almost lost her breath at the frigid impact with the water. 'Twas beyond cold, but still refreshingly so. After breaking the surface, she treaded water and called, "'Tis wonderful, and you're missing out."

With his gaze on hers, he advanced. "I believe the last time we swam together would have been in the loch near my old tree hut."

"Aye, that's right." It had been a year since she'd last visited Colin and her mother's kin at Duart Castle on Mull. Colin had skipped his afternoon duties one day and taken her down to the sea. Together they'd swum, him powering through the water with such skilled ease and she being as sly as she could to keep up.

"Bet I can still catch you. Swim. Fast." He flashed a smile full of challenge, then ran and dove.

A wave rippled toward her. She ducked her head, tossed her feet into the air and went under. Kicking toward the center of the pool, she remained below, her lungs near to bursting. Surely, he'd think she'd—

A hand clamped around her ankle and Colin dragged her upward.

She broke the surface in a slew of bubbles and gulped in great breaths.

"Too easy. That white sark you're wearing is like a flag under the water." His gaze was wolfish, his hands on her hips sending a thrill through her.

"Then close your eyes as you should have afore you dove in. Give me time to get away." She shoved a wave of water at him.

He fell back, shook his dark head and sent a spray of drops flying. "So that's how 'twill be."

"Always."

"I'll give you a minute head-start to hide." He lunged and she squealed and kicked backward. "Starting now. One." He closed his eyes.

She was off, kicking with fast strokes toward the stone ledge at the far end. If she could climb on top then she'd be able to hide where it dipped out of sight to the side. He'd never look for her out of the water.

Her sark swirled around her legs, hindering her a touch when she usually only wore an old shirt in the water, but still, she should be able to make that ledge before her minute was up.

"Sixty," Colin yelled.

"Nay, you cheated." He'd counted to ten and no more. She was certain of it.

His golden eyes shone with laughter as he caught up and passed her. She nabbed his feet and held on. Using his arms alone, he powered them both the last twenty feet to the wide overhanging ledge. Then with his hands on the rock, he hauled himself up, reached down and lifted her onto the flat stone beside him. "You've always been a tricky lass. Were you going to hide up here?"

"How could you even think I would?" Water dripped from her dangling feet into the loch.

"Because I know you too well." He caught her hand and pressed it against his thumping heartbeat. "Spending such time with you is always tiring."

"Yet you love it." He'd been her closest kin growing up, and they'd had so much fun, no matter the years separating them. Gently, she spread her fingers over his solid muscle. His wet shirt, almost transparent, showed a smattering of dark chest hair. She slid one finger into the gap between two loosened ties and as his muscles flexed under her touch, a strange heat surged through her.

Now she'd touched him, she couldn't stop, and since he hadn't moved to halt her, she trailed her finger down over each of his rigid abs and swished along his trim waist. Oh, being this close to him was glorious. New and needy emotions reared to life within her. She wanted, and more.

* * * *

Colin's heartbeat thumped as Annie's blue eyes darkened and her breathing quickened. Her wet sark was pressed against her chest, showing the roundness of her full breasts and a tease of pink nipple. The sight sent wicked thoughts racing through his mind, although thoughts he wasn't permitted to have.

He closed his eyes, shoved what he'd seen into the darkest recesses of his mind then opened his eyes and grabbed her wayward hand. She was his ward, and had been since her father had passed away three years ago. "Annie, stop."

"Please, no' yet." She wriggled her fingers free and let them drift over his belly.

"We're cousins." Damn it. He had to stop her before she encountered his rising cock.

"Nay, our grandparents were cousins. We're far removed from being first cousins."

"Third cousins still shouldnae touch each other so."

"Then you might like to inform the king, because there's currently no law against it."

Ever since she'd lost her parents, she'd sought comfort from him on a greater level, and he'd done all he could to provide whatever she'd needed. Except she was no longer a child and as her guardian, he had a responsibility to ensure her future was secured. To the right man, and that would never be him when he had to lead his clan during this current feud. Aye, he needed to push her away, except they'd always been so close, their bond one he adored. Hurting her was impossible. Tenderly, he caught her face in his hands, traced his thumbs over the dusting of freckles covering her tiny nose and cheeks. "I'm no' the man for you, but I will aid you in searching for one. Tell me what you're looking for in a husband."

"In truth, I'd like someone just like you." She skimmed her hands over his. "I'd also love to return to my MacLean roots and be closer to you and my kin. If you're adamant there is naught between us, then I would like a man from Mull."

"You dinnae wish a husband of rank? You can only find that here at court."

"Rank means little when it is what's inside a person that counts." She released him and tapped her chin. "Hmm, what of Arthur?"

"My second isnae looking for a wife when the last lass who took his fancy married another." A small lie, but he'd never be able to stand aside and watch his right-hand man wed her. "He's also here to aid me, no' to woo the lasses."

"Of course. I'm sorry. How long until the king approves your request for a visit with Lachlan? You said yesterday you were waiting."

"That all depends on how accommodating the king is. With the feuds raging, he has little patience with the MacLeans."

"Then you need to be careful and no' aggravate him. I dinnae want you being thrown behind bars right along with your chief."

"I'll be careful, but should I end up in the cells, I expect you to come and visit me."

A teasing smile lifted her lips. "I guess I could bring you your daily bread and water."

"Imp." He swung her into his arms and tossed her into the loch with a resounding splash.

She came up spluttering and laughing, her waist-length hair floating like a lily pad of white-blond around her. "Are you using your strength against me again, Colin MacLean?"

"You need to learn when to hold your tongue."

"I was trained to banter at a very young age, and by the very best. You." Her gaze traveled down his body and she gasped.

Hell. He plucked his wet shirt from his groin, but his stiffened cock was still easy to see. Just when he'd diverted her mind, now he'd gone and brought her thoughts roaring right back on him.

"Colin?" She jerked forward, swam to the ledge and held out her arms for him to lift her up. "Please."

Why couldn't she be like the other lasses and more reserved in her manner? An interrogation was sure to come. He hunkered down, gripped her hands and lifted her. Gently, he set her on her feet beside him as he remained standing. "I want you to forget what you just saw."

"I should, but…" She swayed closer, grazing his chest with her hard nipples. "If you feel aught toward me then we need to speak of it."

"Nay, I feel naught but the love of one cousin for another." His heart ached at the mistruth, but speaking honestly on this subject would do neither of them any good, not when he'd chosen to live by his sword as the captain of his chief's guard. She deserved far more than a warrior whose death might come at any time.

"Do you truly speak the truth? I willnae abide any lies between us."

"Neither will I, and I've no reason to lie to you." And now 'twas time to end this conversation before things between them led down an irreversible path. He strode along the ledge toward the bank. "'Twill be dark soon and we need to return afore you're missed. Should Rory discover you've left the palace on your own, he'll send out a search party."

"Nay, he'll know I'm with you." She chased after him. "I'm no' done talking with you, Colin."

"What we need to do is to find you a man who can handle your constant need to talk." He bounded onto the grassy bank and held out his hands. "Jump."

She did and he caught and swung her down next to him. "Stop jesting with me."

"I'll aid you this eve in finding the right man." He led her to her clothes then dressed as quickly as he could. "It willnae be an easy task, but I'll manage it, somehow."

"You are a stubborn man, third cousin of mine." She wrung her hem then donned her burgundy gown and jacket over top of her wet underclothes.

"Thank you." He ran his fingers through her long locks, tidying her hair as best he could.

"That wasnae a compliment, you dolt." She grasped her skirts and tramped back down the thin forest trail toward the palace.

Hell, he desperately wanted to drag her into his arms and see what their future could possibly hold, but instead he allowed her to walk ahead until they emerged from the woods and the thick stone walls of Holyrood House rose like an impenetrable fortress in the descending dark.

Ahead of him, Annie hastened toward the two-story gatehouse where battlements topped fortified walls and guardsmen patrolled the barbican. Beyond the arch, the northwest tower housing King James VI's apartments rose high and overlooked all. The king who'd imprisoned his chief, and the king he sought an audience with.

He caught Annie up, and with a hand on her lower back, steered her across the inner courtyard toward the side entrance near the service quarters. 'Twas best they bypassed the great hall and surrounding rooms which would be abuzz with people so close to the dinner hour. The less people who saw their damp hair and clothing, the better.

Annie slipped through the open doors and peeked down the corridor. "'Tis clear. I didnae realize 'twas so late. Aunt Elizabeth will have already left her chamber and joined the guests for the evening meal."

"Then we'll change quickly and find her." He led her down the gloomy passageway lit by the odd candle in an iron wall sconce. Along the darkest section, he stopped outside her paneled door next to her aunt's chamber and nodded at her. "I'll wait here."

Annie tipped her ear up. "I hear something."

The heavy clomp of booted feet traveled toward him.

Quickly, he nudged her out of sight into the recessed alcove beside her door. "Shh," he whispered in her ear. "No' a noise."

"I cannae believe you lost track of the MacLeod chit in the woods. I gave you one simple task, to follow her," a man rasped as he stormed past them with another man, their tall, shadowed bodies blending into the dark.

"I watched her for a mite," the other man said, "until she stumbled upon MacLean and the two vanished into the woods. I couldnae find where either of them had gone."

"Are they talking about me?" Annie hushed as she slid her hands around his waist and tucked her head under his chin.

"Aye." Colin wrapped his arms around her as the men disappeared around the far corner. "This is what I've been warning you about. Your cousin is the Chief of MacLeod. Not only is he deeply favored by the king, but any alliance formed with you brings with it Rory's might." Frustration burned through him. "Did you recognize their voices?"

"Nay." She stared down the corridor. "And 'twas too dark to see. You should follow them, discover who they are. There's time if you hurry."

"I cannae leave you alone after what I just heard. If there is one man seeking you, there could well be another. All here are aware you seek a husband." He opened her door and stopped in the pitch black. "Why has your maid has no' lit your fire or a candle?"

"I told her that could wait until I retired for bed. I thought I'd be back in plenty of time to dress afore it got dark."

"Wait here. I'll find us some light." He strode down the hallway to the last lit candle, collected it and returned. Annie stood shivering and rubbing her chilled arms. He set the candle in the holder on her side table and ushered her across to her curtained ambry. "Choose something warm and change, as quickly as you can."

"Is your tunic drying out, or will you need another for the

evening meal?" She selected a pale blue gown and stepped behind the silk dressing screen next to her four-poster bed with its sweeping navy velvet canopy and golden tassels.

"I'll need to change." Although, he wouldn't be leaving her alone, not after what he'd heard in the hallway. "We'll stay together."

"When the maid returned with my laundry this morn, by accident she left one of Rory's tunics behind. Rory will never know if you wish to borrow it. It'd save you a trip to your chamber."

"Aye, I'd appreciate it." Changing here would be far more preferable than having to sneak her to his wing which housed so many of the single men.

"You'll find his tunic on top of my trunk under the window."

"I see it." He tugged off his shirt, donned the white tunic and retied his black doublet.

"It appears I shall need a hand." Annie stepped out from behind the screen holding her gown's low-cut silk neckline to her chest. The full swell of her breasts rose on a deep inhale as she turned and gave him her back. Over her shoulder, she smiled. "You dinnae mind?"

"I'm no maid but I'll manage." Bare skin, so creamy and smooth, beckoned. He brushed aside her glossy blond locks, picked up the ties and laced the stays as quickly as he could. Finished, he ran her comb through her hair until the pale strands curled around his fingers like a silken web. "You're presentable."

Now they needed to go. His desire for her deepened with each moment they spent together, something he couldn't allow.

Finding her a husband was imperative, and soon.

* * * *

Annie wandered down the passageway, Colin at her side and his crisp outdoor scent swirling around her, a delectable tease of pine and fresh water she'd always adored.

"What has that smile on your face?" He pressed a hand to her lower back and warm tingles raced across her skin.

"Thoughts of you." If only she had more time to choose a husband, but Rory expected her to secure an engagement before they left Holyrood.

"You shouldnae be thinking of me." Colin stopped at the entrance to the great hall.

She took a deep, fortifying breath. The massive vaulted room held a sweeping crown of rafters rising to an impressive height more similar to a small cathedral. Beautiful tapestries, of hunting and landscape scenes, hung with pride around the vast room filled with a merry and hungry crowd. "Well, finding Aunt Elizabeth and Rory in this gathering willnae be an easy task."

"But find them we will. Come." Colin weaved around the perimeter and she followed in his path around the mingling groups. A serving girl approached with a tray and he accepted two goblets of wine, handed her one then continued on through the doors leading into a side room where pipers played a lively tune.

Music flowed around her as she sipped. "Can you see them?"

"Nay, no' yet. Mayhap we should eat afore attempting a more in-depth search." He stopped before a side table with a white embroidered tablecloth fluttering in the breeze from the open balcony doors. The table was laden with platters of meat and succulent roasted vegetables. Colin set his goblet down and selected a sugared plum, one of her favorite fruits. "Try this." He slipped it between her lips.

The sweet ripeness burst over her tongue and she licked his trailing fingertip, not wanting to miss a drop of the delicious juice. "Mmm, wonderful."

He groaned and cleared his throat. "Next time you can feed yourself."

She grinned. "All I heard was next time."

"Good evening." Arthur, Colin's right-hand man, eased past a group of guests and joined them. Wearing a forest-green silk tunic and black leather trews, the striking colors matched his vivid green gaze and midnight-black hair to perfection. "Annie, you're looking bonny this eve."

"Thank you. And you look dangerously dashing."

"Ah, lass, you'll make me blush." He took her hand and pressed a kiss against her knuckles.

"Enough." Colin knocked Arthur's shoulder. "No dallying with Annie when you're still distressed about the lass you lost."

"What lass is that?" Arthur frowned, his expression perplexed.

Oh, Colin had been telling fibs again. Well, two could play at that game. She set her goblet down and faced Arthur. The warrior stroked the hilt of his belted sword and the blade swayed and glinted in the candlelight. Aye, Arthur appealed, and she'd always felt so protected whether he or Colin were nearby. Certainly the man's towering height and powerful bearing showcased the depth of his MacLean ancestry, that of their Gaelic clan born of a king. Arthur had also always had a kind word for her. "How have you been of late, Arthur?"

"Better if our chief were no' locked behind bars."

Colin rested his hand on her lower back, stroked his thumb in a small circle. "Aye, I'm still awaiting word on when I may see Lachlan, but I hope soon."

Unable to help herself, she inched closer to Colin. His little touches always soothed her. "Why is the king taking so long to approve a visit?"

"He inserts his control, and none may gainsay him." Colin eyed his man. "We've been looking for Rory and Elizabeth. Have you by chance seen either of them this eve?"

"I passed Elizabeth only a moment ago." He motioned over Annie's shoulder toward a group of chattering women.

Her aunt's back was to her, but her unmistakable auburn hair, piled high atop her head, gave proof 'twas her. "Oh, how did I miss her?" She squeezed Colin's arm. "Stay and talk to Arthur. I willnae be long. I must see my aunt so she knows I've arrived."

"A sound idea. Save your first dance for me."

"I will." She clutched her skirts and eased around the dancers toward Elizabeth.

"Well, well, if it isnae Annie MacLeod." James MacDonald, attired in a great plaid fastened across his chest with a silver pin, stepped directly into her path. "You're the very lass I was after."

"James, how are you?" She fluttered her hand over her chest. Goodness, should Colin see her with his greatest enemy, a battle would certainly ensue.

"I'm well, but you've not yet been to Dunscaith Castle to see Anne." He crossed his arms and lifted one bushy red eyebrow. "My brother's new wife misses you."

"As I miss Anne, but I thought it best to give her some time to settle into her new home and married life afore I asked Rory if a visit might be permissible." Something she had no idea how she'd arrange when the relationship between their clans was so on edge. A truce had been achieved by the marriage of one of her kin, Anne MacLeod to Alex MacDonald, but 'twas still a very uneasy truce. "How is Anne?"

"Enjoying wedded bliss, as is my brother. 'Tis why I've come to Holyrood House in Alex's stead. Tearing him away from his wife right now would be impossible."

With Donald, his chief and uncle, currently in the cells, James would also be here for the same reason as Colin, to see his laird. Certainly no warrior left his chief to fight his battles alone.

"I'm also here because you are, Annie."

"Pardon?"

"Word reached me on Skye that you'd traveled to court to

seek a husband. Is the king still demanding you make a significant match?" Dozens of candles in the circular overhead chandelier highlighted the spark of interest in James's eyes.

"Aye, but this time the choice is mine, a wish Rory granted me." She and James had spoken honestly with each other during her short stay at Dunscaith.

"I'm glad." He glanced over her head and snorted. "Colin MacLean appears rather disturbed we're talking. It might pay for us to take this conversation to where we cannae be interrupted. Would you care to dance?"

"I was just on my way to see my—"

"Wonderful." He swung her onto the floor as a new reel started.

"James, what are you doing?"

"Proving that not all the MacDonalds and MacLeods enjoy warring. Smile, otherwise MacLean will take my head off if he thinks you didnae wish to join me."

"You're playing with fire." Still, she didn't intend to be the catalyst for Colin calling James out, so she planted a smile on her face and curtsied as another couple joined them and they formed a small circle.

"I like fire, but I also like a woman with spirit, and that trait you have in abundance." He caught her hands and moved her through the steps to the energetic tune.

A low growl sounded from close behind and she shivered as Colin made his displeasure more than known. To James, she whispered, "You'd best speak of what's on your mind afore the song ends."

"There is naught like a little rivalry to light a fire under a MacLean." He grinned, clearly enjoying himself.

"James." She wanted to slap him. "Speak now, or I shall leave you on this floor to fend off Colin on your own."

He chuckled but nodded. "Aye, you and I have always enjoyed each other's company which is unusual for those within our warring clans, and it's that friendship that now leads me to what I'd like to ask of you. Annie, if you're in need of a proposal, then I'd like you to consider forming an alliance with me. I realize you never wished to wed my brother, but 'tis time for me to take a wife and a marriage between the two of us would further strengthen the ties between our clans. When Anne wed Alex, it helped ease some of the immediate tension, but these are difficult times and unless the clans join more fully together, further unrest will only prevail."

Had he just proposed to her in the middle of the dance floor?

"Lass, dinnae look so shocked." He twirled her around and sent her pale blue skirts flying. "All I ask is that you take some time to consider my proposal, and while you do, allow me to court you. I simply ask for a fair chance at your hand."

Could she marry James? Aye, he'd been kind and considerate to her during her stay at the MacDonald stronghold while awaiting her handfast to his brother at the king's demand, and their friendship had remained strong since, but he was still Colin's enemy. "I'm no' sure."

Concern furrowed his brow. "Have you received another offer?"

"Nay."

"Then allow me to court you."

"That would be as good as saying aye to your proposal since a courtship usually leads to an engagement."

"Yet you must procure an engagement while you're here."

"An alliance has still been made between our clans because of Anne. She is a MacLeod and married to your brother."

"Anne has no direct tie to Rory, only you do. There is also the fact your mother was a MacLean. With both you and Anne living at Dunscaith Castle, there will finally be a chance for this feud to ease between all three clans. 'Tis time for the MacDonalds, MacLeods and MacLeans to cease fighting. Help me bring a resolution to all the years of fierce warring. Between you and I, we could do so."

She couldn't deny the truth in his statement, and marrying for such a reason would be an honorable thing to do. "You're quite serious?"

"Very." He grinned. "On the morrow, come riding with me. We shall speak more then."

"I would like that." Colin wouldn't, but then her choices were so limited.

"I'll meet you at the stables after you've had time to break your fast." He dipped his head.

"Aye, on the morrow."

"Thank you for agreeing." He pressed a kiss to her hand and walked away.

"What the hell did James want?" Colin rasped as he slid in behind her, his chest a solid wall of heat at her back.

"Dinnae be angry." She spun around.

"Speak. I'll have no secrets between us."

"He wishes to form an alliance and build the bonds between our clans."

"What kind of an alliance?" His golden eyes burned with fury.

"Surely you can imagine considering the reason why I'm here."

"He intends to offer for you?"

"Aye, he made his position clear."

"And so will I." He leaned in until his nose brushed hers. "You're no' to go near him again, and I will make certain of it. Do we understand each other?"

She surely did, but perhaps Colin had forgotten she had a mind of her own.

"Damn it. You're no' listening. I can see that defiant spark in your eyes. We need to talk, and somewhere where we'll be afforded more privacy." He guided her through the balcony doors and into the cool night air.

Aye, they would talk, and she didn't doubt this was one conversation she wouldn't care for.

Chapter 2

Colin stormed down the steps and along the pebbled path twisting through the trees, his hold on Annie's hand firm.

"Slow down, Colin."

"MacDonald touched you."

"That happens when couples dance."

"You're no' a couple." He strode around a thick trunk and thumped it with his fist. "He touched you, and I could do naught about it."

"I'm sorry." Breathing hard, she caught his other hand before he could hit the tree again. "'Twas just a dance." She squeezed his fingers. "One single dance."

"I said I'd aid you in choosing a husband, but it'll never be him." Hell, her soft touch scorched him like a brand. He pressed her against the tree and planted his hands either side of her head. Looking into her beautiful eyes, he allowed his anger to dispel. "I'd never hurt you, but I'd kill to keep you safe. Make no mistake about that."

"This feud between the clans must come to an end. Times are changing and I have a chance to make a difference. Please, make no mistake about that." She smoothed her hands over his chest. "I have no' said aye to James, but only agreed to see where things might lead. I'm still very open to anyone you might suggest a match with. Give me some choices."

"I need time." He pulled her into his arms, tucked her cheek against his chest and breathed in her intoxicating rose scent.

"Something I'm running out of."

"I'm well aware, but you need a husband who understands how much love you have to give, that you thrive when your clan remains close by. A MacDonald cannae provide that when we're at war with them." Gently, he stroked down her sides and over the soft swell of her hips. He shouldn't touch her so, except he couldn't help himself, not after what he'd witnessed on the dance floor. He wanted to rip MacDonald's arms from his sockets and slice his head from his shoulders. Aye, and he still might.

"Colin?" She lifted her head and met his gaze, her eyes deep pools of midnight-blue he wanted to drown in. "I'm used to you touching me, but no' quite like this."

"I'm simply comforting you." He had no control over his emotions right now. All he wanted to do was to lower his head, take her mouth with his and kiss her as he'd secretly desired for three long years. If only she didn't tempt him beyond his endurance, except this day, she'd unleashed the deepest craving he'd ever suffered. Now, desperate emotions warred within him as everything about her called to him. "I'm your guardian and I will remain so."

Words he needed to tell himself over and over to make certain they stuck.

"So you've already told me. Speak to me." She reached up on her toes and brushed her soft lips across his cheek. Temptation warred within him. If he turned his head a fraction, their lips would meet.

"This is one issue I dare no' speak of. For both our sakes."

"If there's a chance there could be something more between us, then tell me."

"There's naught." Firm words, yet he didnae mean them,

no' one bit.

"Annie! There you are," Elizabeth called as she hurried down the path toward them. She swamped Annie in a hug, her navy skirts swishing around her. "I've been unable to find you all afternoon, and then I caught sight of you and Colin leaving the great hall. Are you well?"

"Very." Annie hugged her back. "Colin needed some fresh air and requested my company. We spent the afternoon in the park."

"That sounds lovely." Elizabeth patted his arm. "Thank you, Colin. That's wonderful of you to escort Annie while I napped. Oh, and afore I forget. Rory wished a word. He's waiting for you inside."

"I wish a word with him too." He extended an arm to each of the ladies, glad for Elizabeth's well-timed interruption. Another minute and he might well have given into Annie.

"I'll walk ahead. This path is rather narrow." Elizabeth waved off his offer, gripped her skirts and headed back toward the great hall.

"Annie." He nodded for her to accept.

"Thank you." She slid her fingers through his crooked elbow and a buzz of awareness tingled his fingers and toes. If he could just stop touching her all would be well, and if he could get rid of James MacDonald, even more so.

He strolled inside with Elizabeth leading the way around the crowded dance floor. Rory stood near the king's hefty silver shield hanging in a pride of place along the far wall. Annie released him, adjusted the long sleeves of her pale blue gown edged with white lace and joined her chief and cousin.

"Good evening, Annie." Rory grinned and tweaked her chin. "How has your day been?"

"Wonderful. I took a walk in the park and caught up with Colin. How have your discussions with the king gone?"

"There were several other clan chiefs present today, and the talks became rather tense, something I wish to speak to Colin about." Smile gone, he gripped Colin's shoulder. "The king demands an end to the feuds which rampage throughout Scotland, but few of the others are listening, no' while he holds your chief and Donald and Angus MacDonald in the tower. The knowledge he's tossed three mighty chiefs into the cells does no' sit well with the other clan chiefs. The king grows frustrated by it all."

"Thank you for the warning. I'm still awaiting the king's permission to visit Lachlan, but once I'm permitted in, I'll pass on your words."

"James MacDonald also made the same request this afternoon, to visit with Donald." Rory slid his gaze to Annie. "A man I've no' long since seen you with. Do you care to explain?"

"As I told Colin, we enjoyed a dance. I am here to find a husband."

"You need to steer well clear of the MacDonalds." Rory drummed one foot. "Listen well, Annie. The feud between us and James's clan might have recently eased due to their chief being locked away, but you're no longer tied to them through a possible handfast. I need you to choose swiftly, but wisely."

"There is also time, Annie." Elizabeth opened her fan and fluttered it. "And plenty of men here at court for you to choose from. Goodness, this is such a dour conversation to be having when we should be enjoying ourselves. Mayhap some dancing would lighten our moods." She tapped Colin's arm with her fan. "What do you say, my boy?"

Only Elizabeth could get away with calling him a boy. He almost grinned, but instead he bowed his head toward her. "That sounds lovely. Would you care to dance, my lady?"

"You naughty boy." She giggled. "I didnae mean with me but with Annie."

"Aunt Elizabeth." Annie gasped. "You're the naughty one." She glanced at him. "I'm sure you wish to speak to Rory some more. We can dance when you're done."

"Aye, but you promised me your first dance and since you didnae keep your word, you owe me the next two." It wasn't the best idea to dance with her when his emotions still ran amok, but the image of James on the floor with her wouldn't leave his mind and the only way to dispel it was to replace it with one of himself. "Please, will you dance with me?"

A blush crept across her cheeks. "I'd like that."

He led her across the floor and she curtsied, her gown's square-cut neckline dipping and exposing the top milky swell of her breasts. She had the most gloriously smooth skin.

"So, Colin MacLean, what are your true intentions?" She danced forward and around him.

"Ah, whatever do you mean?"

"About your chief. I know you, and you'll never allow Lachlan to remain behind bars for long."

"Aye, but 'tis best I dinnae share my plans regarding Lachlan with you."

"I knew it." She narrowed her blue gaze and popped out her tiny chin, one stubborn chin he wished desperately to kiss. "You're going to free him should the king no' let him go. Am I right?"

"Shh, I dinnae need that kind of gossip spreading." She was too clever by far. "Remember your promise, scamp."

"What promise?"

"To keep clear of James."

"I promised no such thing, and dinnae try to turn this conversation back on me." She searched the room. "Mayhap I should dance with Arthur instead. Your second has kind eyes and a sweeter disposition than you."

"There is naught sweet about the man, and he has the eyes of a hawk."

"Is he no' preferable to James as a husband?" She swept around him then back. "He's so gallant."

Every muscle in his body tensed. After he killed James, he'd kill Arthur.

"Goodness, where is your concentration this eve?" She frowned and caught his hands. "You're standing still when we're supposed to be moving in a circle."

"My concentration disappeared when you said Arthur was gallant. The man is too old for you."

"He's the same age as you, which is a far more acceptable age than Lord Sinclare's seventy years. I have so little time, and you need to stop finding fault with every man I might choose."

"Then I'll speak to Arthur." He wouldn't, not when he'd be forced to bear witness to their union on a daily basis should she marry him. That he could never—hell. Easing around the dancers, Arthur headed his way. His man motioned for him to leave the floor.

"It appears I'm needed." He steered Annie toward Arthur but kept a firm hand at her back. "What's happened?" he asked Arthur.

"One of the king's men requested I find you. You've been given approval to visit Lachlan. This eve."

Finally. This was the news he'd been waiting for, except he'd given Annie his word he'd help her.

"'Twill be all right." Annie nodded in understanding. "You can aid me on the morrow, which might be better at any rate. Hopefully your head will have cleared of all your disapproving thoughts by then."

"Those thoughts will never clear unless you cease putting them there."

"You're impossible." She giggled and the sweet sound eased a touch of his frustration. He adored her laugh and had since the moment he'd first heard it escape her lips as a babe in her mother's arms. She found such joy in everything she did.

"Something you shouldnae forget." He tipped her chin up and looked into her eyes. He couldn't believe what he was about to say. "Stay with Arthur. I want your promise on that."

"I promise."

Voice low, he said to Arthur, "Two men were following her earlier this afternoon, although I've yet to discover who they were. If Annie wishes to return to her chamber, then remain outside until I arrive. I want her guarded at all times."

"Aye, Captain. I'll be happy to escort the lass wherever she needs to go." Arthur grinned at Annie. "My lady, would you care to dance?"

"Why thank you. That would be lovely." She took his offered arm, and Colin grit his teeth and forced himself to walk away.

These irrational thoughts had to go.

He was here to free his chief, not to dance with Annie.

* * * *

After taking a turn with Arthur, Annie danced with several men, one after the other until her feet ached and her head swam. As the midnight hour struck and she could dance no more, she joined her aunt and Arthur as they waited attentively at the edge of the hall.

"Any new prospects, my dear?" Elizabeth asked as she fluttered her delicate white silk fan. "What did you think of the Campbell chief's nephew?"

"He was pleasant." Although none of the men had kept her interest when her thoughts had returned to Colin and his meeting with his chief. "I'm rather tired. It might pay for me to consider my prospects once I've had a good night's rest."

"A sound idea."

"If you ladies are ready to retire, then allow me to escort you back to your chambers." Arthur motioned toward the passageway.

"Wonderful." Elizabeth linked her arm through Annie's and they weaved through the throng with Arthur close behind.

At her aunt's door, Annie bid her a goodnight then leaned

against her own door, her hands tucked between her and the solid wood as she faced Arthur. "Colin's opinion is rather biased at the moment, but I'm curious to learn what you might think of James? James is certain any match made between us will help ease the feud between the clans."

"Possibly, but he still plays with your emotions as only a MacDonald can do, and I've no doubt he'll use any alliance he made with you against Colin." He squeezed her shoulder. "Dinnae give up on Colin. He cares for you, and far more than he's ready to acknowledge, to you or himself."

"His mind is set, that there is naught between us."

"His mind is in chaos." He leaned forward and brushed a kiss against her forehead. "You and I are kin, and should you need an engagement that's breakable, I'd be happy to oblige. There's no need for you to tie yourself to a MacDonald when you need to remain close to your own kin."

"You'd truly marry me?"

"Aye, though I'm certain Colin would never allow us to truly speak vows. His stubborn resolve would break afore then."

"I dinnae want to break him." She tapped the door softly then pushed away from it. "Thank you for your kind offer, but I dinnae wish to cause any friction between the two of you and that would happen should I agree."

"Any friction would be well worth it." He opened her door. "Think on my offer. 'Twill remain open until you've made your decision. Sleep well, Annie." He eased back into the darkened recess and blended in with the shadows.

"Goodnight, Arthur." She walked inside and shut her door. Well, two proposals in one night, except neither from the man she truly wished had asked.

"There you are, my lady." Maggie dusted her hands against her aproned sides as she rose from before the crackling fire. "Would you like help readying yourself for bed?"

"Aye, I would. 'Tis been a long day."

Maggie loosened the back ties of her gown and after she stepped out of it, hung it in the navy curtained ambry.

"There's a tunic on top of my trunk that needs laundering. A keepsake. One of my father's." 'Twas the only way to explain why she had Colin's shirt, a man's shirt, in her chamber. She removed her sark and tugged her nightrail over her head. "Take care with it and return it once it's laundered."

She collected the shirt. "Will that be all?"

"Aye, rest well. I'll see you in the morn."

The girl bobbed her head and left.

The night would grow colder, but for now, the fire spread its delicious warmth throughout the stone chamber. She crawled under the covers and snuggled as thoughts of Colin flittered through her mind. Outside under the tree, he'd touched her so intimately. What did it all mean when he'd insisted he thought of her as a cousin and no more? Had he lied?

It might pay to speak to Elizabeth about things. Her aunt was as understanding as her mother had always been, and she and Elizabeth had become so close of late. Aye, she missed her mother, the woman who'd shown her how wonderful love could be. She and her father had married to bring their two clans closer together, MacLeod and MacLean, but in doing so they'd fallen in love and known such happiness in their years together. That's what she wanted, to do the best by her clan but also to strike the right match.

If only there wasn't such unrest in the Highlands. When the clans denied the king what he wished, they soon found disfavor and bounties on their heads and so many warriors had lost their lands once cast out. Those warriors then took what they wanted, where they wanted, and it had been just such a band of highly trained men who'd attacked her parents' party as they'd traveled on a short trip north from Dunvegan to the tip of Skye. That day, her father had died protecting her and Mother.

Her gaze misted and she shoved back the unwanted tears.

Mother had fought her captor and hit her head on a low tree branch as the brigands had marched them through the forest, and during the week they'd been held for ransom in the leader's camp awaiting Rory's payment, the woman she'd loved with all her heart had never fully woken from the blow.

Rory though had not waited for the exchange of coin. He and Colin had broken the messenger, discovered their location and stormed into camp. That day would be forever etched in her mind. Colin had slashed his way through the outlaws to reach her while Rory had gone berserk and killed every single warrior in his path. Not one of the men in camp had been granted leniency for slaying her father, and 'twas a strong message Rory had sent that day, that none would ever attack his clan so again.

If only Rory and Colin had come in time for Mother. She'd held Mother's hand as she lay unresponsive on her dusty plaid, and when she'd kissed her mother's cheek and told her Colin had come, her mother's fingers had fluttered over hers and she'd breathed her last. Losing both her parents within days of each other had near torn her heart in two. She'd only survived the ordeal because of Colin.

In the weeks that had followed, he'd held her each night and mourned with her as she'd cried herself to sleep. How was ever supposed to live without him when she wed? Certainly if she gave James's proposal the due consideration it required, any marriage with him would take her away from Colin and Rory.

She closed her eyes and a tear escaped.

As much as she adored Arthur for his proposal, it had been made for one reason only, to force Colin's hand. That she couldn't do.

* * * *

Colin strode into the tower after waiting until midnight for the guards to finally allow him clear passage through. With his weapons removed and stored in the guards' antechamber, an edgy frustration sizzled through him.

The guardsman led the way up the winding stairwell. The walls were tight and Colin's shoulders brushed the blackened stone either side of him. So too he had to duck his head or else knock it on the low rafters above. The tactical design would certainly ensure a man couldn't swing his sword in this area during an attack.

On each darkened landing he passed, a little more room allowed him added movement, although with the narrow windows boarded shut, barely a trace of light passed through. Odorous, musty air clogged his throat. Lachlan had been living in these conditions for weeks and that sent his anger soaring. The king treated Lachlan like the worst scourge instead of the great chief he was.

"This way." The warrior, his hand firm on his belted side sword, strode down the darkened corridor then halted at a heavily barred door. He turned the lock and pushed the rusty door open with a teeth-grinding screech. "I'll return soon."

"My thanks, but take your time." He entered the stone cell lit by a single candle burning in an iron wall sconce.

"You have ten minutes." The door scraped shut and the lock clunked back into place behind him.

Ahead, Lachlan sat on a dusty pallet, his wrists manacled and chained to the wall. His ragged tunic and trews hung off him.

Kneeling at his chief's feet, he grasped Lachlan's forearms in a firm warrior's hold. "You look terrible."

"'Tis good to see you too, Colin." He cleared his raspy throat. "How is my wife?"

"Margaret is furious you got caught, and Hector is determined to slay the king even though at seven, he cannae lift a sword."

"My son is no different to me at this moment then. I too cannae lift a sword." He rattled his chains. "Does Calum hold Duart Castle?"

"Aye, and he willnae allow it to fall." He picked up a grimy pitcher from the floor and poured murky water into a chipped tankard and held it to Lachlan's chapped lips.

After taking a hearty swallow, Lachlan mumbled, "Donald and Angus MacDonald are in the cells at the end of the corridor. You'll have to keep your voice down so we're no' overheard."

Nodding, he pulled the linen-wrapped meat he'd pilfered from the great hall out of his pocket. The thick slabs of beef, even though cold, still seasoned the stuffy air. Lachlan took a deep whiff and Colin tore a sliver and fed him. "Eat slowly."

"Good man," he mumbled as he ate. "You should visit more often."

"I'd rather you no' be here to visit." At least his chief appeared undefeated.

"I wish that too."

"How do the talks go between you and the king?"

"He's being unreasonable, insisting the MacDonalds and I pay hefty fines, which he calls arrears in lieu of duties and crown rents. He also wishes to ascertain our future obedience with the enforcement of certain conditions. Apparently all of us must cease opposing the government and when summoned to Edinburgh, return within twenty days or he and the Privy Council will declare us outlaws and have our lands forfeited. Donald and Angus are furious. And so am I." His gaze narrowed until the whites remained barely visible. "Now you're here, 'tis time for me to leave. I will battle the king from my own land where I can stand strong."

His chief's request didn't surprise him, and he'd come fully prepared.

"Arthur is here at the palace with me, while Ian and Murdock wait in the forest. I brought our best."

"Good." Lachlan ate another bite of meat and after chewing, continued, "You'll need to keep an eye on the sentry. There are four of them guarding this tower and they change at midnight and midday. I'm afraid all are loyal to the king, so you'll get no aid from that quarter, but I'll be waiting, no matter the hour or day."

"I'll return the night of the masquerade, only a few days hence. The ball will offer the perfect diversion for your escape."

The key clanked and he tucked the cloth that had held the meat back into his pocket. "It appears my time is up." He grasped Lachlan's arm. "Virtue mine honor."

"Aye, Colin. By death or life, I will stand firm."

The guardsman entered and motioned Colin forward. He left as mocking sniggers echoed from the MacDonalds down the corridor. They would pay for their part in this atrocity, and he'd make certain of it.

At the guards' station, he collected his weapons then stepped outside into the fresh evening air. Time was running out. He had a chief to free, Annie to find a husband for, and two unidentified men to locate and apprehend. That last threat gnawed furiously inside him. He'd never allow anyone to hurt Annie. She was his to protect, his to care for, and always had been.

In the dark of the night, he jogged across the inner courtyard, eager to return to her even though the hour was late and she'd likely be abed. Outside her door, he stopped as Arthur slid out of the shadowed recess. "How is she?" he asked his man.

"There have been no disturbances, and she remains alone. I can stay for the night if you wish."

"Nay. I'll keep guard."

"What of Lachlan?"

"His discussions with the king go nowhere and he awaits his rescue. Since I'm to meet Ian at The White Dover Inn in the morn, I'll confirm with him the mission will take place at midnight on the night of the masquerade. I'll need you to remain here watching over Annie while I ride into the city. She must be kept safe."

"Aye, I willnae fail you." Arthur clasped his shoulder. "I fear she's considering a match with MacDonald. I offered for her."

"You better damn well no' have."

"She thanked me and turned me down. Think on that. I'll see you in the morn." Arthur disappeared into the dark.

Arthur was too damn observant. Annie was all he'd thought about of late and his man knew it. Only he had no idea what to do about her. Without a snick of noise, he opened the solid paneled door, snuck inside and slid the bolt home.

Keeping to the shadows, he moved soundlessly toward her four-poster bed with its navy canopy and golden-tasseled ties. She slept on her back, her pale blond lashes glimmering in the fire's glow. Quietly, he lowered to his haunches and gently smoothed the back of his knuckles across her flushed cheeks. Everything about her touched his heart, and he desperately wished he could explore what was between them. Except taking that chance when his current mission was such a treacherous one, would only endanger her.

He breathed deep and her sweet rose scent swirled seductively around him. Her mother had adored roses, and she and Annie had planted cuttings along the forest path near their cottage. Wild copses of roses had bloomed, and each time he'd ridden that trail over the years and encountered the fragrance, memories of Annie stirred and overwhelmed him. He hated that she lived so far away on the Isle of Skye, that he could only visit her when his duties allowed it. Those visits of late had become fewer and further between.

"Mmm, Colin." She pushed her arms out from under the covers, dislodging the tartan blanket.

Hell. Her nightrail was loose at the top and gaped open.

With shaky hands, he caught the ties, but before he could pull them together, she wriggled and stretched and exposed her full breasts.

"Dinnae leave me, Colin. You promised you'd always be close," she murmured in her sleep.

Lust shot straight to his cock. This had been the most tortuous day, and it appeared it wasn't yet at an end. He needed to close those ties. He hauled the fabric together as best he could and knotted it.

"Colin?" She blinked her eyes open and grasped his hands and sat up. "You're back. Is all well?"

"As well as can be. The king thinks to weaken Lachlan but his mind remains strong."

"The Chief of MacLean is one of the most determined warriors I know. He'll never lose his mind or fail his clan." She wriggled across and patted the mattress. "You look tired. Surely you can guard me from here."

"I should sleep afore the fire." Yet he kicked off his boots, propped his sword beside the bed where it would lay within easy reach and slid in beside her. The itch thrumming through him to be close to her was too strong to be curtailed. "Come here, scamp."

She rolled into his side, slid her hand over his chest. Her soft circular strokes over his heart soothed him, as did her warm lips pressed against his cheek. "You worry too much."

"There are two men intent on harming you. James proposed, and Arthur admitted to me he too made an offer."

"I turned Arthur down, although he didnae take my answer as a firm nay and told me to think on it."

"You cannae wed him." His words, a mere whisper between them, were the strongest he'd ever issued. "I'm sorry, but bearing witness to the two of you together would kill me."

"Why is that?" She kissed the corner of his lips. "Do you feel what could be between us too?"

"I gave my chief an oath, and I must abide by it. I'm here for him, no' to dally with you."

"You dally with no woman, or at least none I've noticed."

She licked along his lower lip and heat surged through his veins. "A point you should take note of."

"Because you continually scatter my thoughts, as you're doing now." He cradled her face in his hands. "Annie, you've held a piece of my heart since the day you were born and always will, but of late, we've grown too close. I want to kiss you, and 'tis wrong."

"What would be wrong is no' kissing me." A teasing smile lifted her lips. "I want to kiss you as well, to know what it's like to share the same breath as you."

"Damn it. You're no' listening."

"Colin." Brow arched, she tapped his mouth. "You shouldnae swear when a lass makes such a request. 'Tis no wonder you're still unwed."

"Which I intend to remain. Warriors have short lives, and you need a man who can care for you throughout all of your days."

"Life is meant to be lived. Kiss me now so I'll no longer wonder what your lips on mine would feel like. You know how curious I can get."

"Such a request could also get you into a world of trouble."

"I like trouble." She threaded her fingers deep into his hair, guided his mouth to hers and kissed him. Her breath whispered softly across his tongue, a teasing caress that had him urging her lips apart to capture more of her essence.

This was wrong, but now he'd indulged, he couldn't stop. Need rushed through him and he took control of the kiss, plunged his tongue inside her mouth and drank in her delectable innocence. He welcomed the raw intimacy, one he'd craved for so long.

"Mmm, I love the feel of your mouth on mine." She pressed her breasts against his chest, kissed his jaw and nibbled toward his ear. "My heart is beating so fast. I'm no' sure what to do."

"I feel your heartbeat." It pounded ruthlessly against his

own. "Annie, what are we doing?"

"Getting into trouble, together. Kiss me again."

"I didnae come in here to ravish you, but to ensure your safety." He had to insert some space between them, to clear his head. "'Tis been a long day and we both need to rest."

"Well, I'm wide awake now."

"I'm exhausted." He tucked her against his side, pulled the covers over them both. "Sleep, scamp. I cannae take any more right now."

"Then we'll sleep. I dinnae want to cause you more worry when you have enough on your shoulders." She snuggled and slowly, her breathing evened out as she drifted.

The moment Annie succumbed to sleep, he finally closed his eyes and allowed his need for rest to take him.

* * * *

Waking to the sensation of Annie sleeping with her leg draped across his lower body and her hand curled around his neck, had Colin's groin tightening. He shouldn't have stayed in her bed, but he'd needed to hold her, and before he no longer had the chance to do so.

Carefully, he extricated himself from her warmth, hauled on his boots and strapped on his sword belt. With dawn so close, 'twas best he left before the rest of the castle stirred.

At the hearth, he prodded the embers back to blazing life and tossed a slab of peat on the fire.

"Is it morning already?" Annie murmured as she propped herself up on her elbows, her pale hair a tangled mess around her shoulders.

"Almost. I have business to be about in the city and the castle will soon awaken. I need you to bolt the door after I leave, and open it only for those you know. I've already instructed Arthur to guard you this day. You're no' to go anywhere without him. I dinnae need to worry about you anymore than I already do." He walked to the door.

"I promise I'll be careful. Will you be gone all day?" Annie hopped across the cold floorboards. "Oh, cold, cold." She jumped onto his booted feet and stopped him in his path. "Sorry, but I usually pull socks on when I get out of bed. You move too fast."

"I'll get them for you."

"Nay, never mind. I'm here now." She wobbled and slid her arms around his waist. "You'll be careful too?"

"Always."

"You kissed me last eve." She smiled, so brightly.

"Aye, and 'twas a nice kiss."

"So you still dinnae wish to talk about us?"

"There is no us."

She tut-tutted then said, "Whenever my father used to leave for the day, he always used to kiss my mother goodbye. He told me 'twas so she remained on his mind all day, as he wished to remain on hers." Challenge lit her stunning blue eyes. "I would like to remain on your mind all day."

"I will always think of you, kisses or no'." He pressed her against the wall, every inch of their bodies fully aligned until heat raced the entire length of his body. How was he supposed to keep control when she teased and tempted him like this? One kiss, but he'd make it quick. He brushed his lips over hers then jerked back. "Done."

"My father kissed my mother with far more passion than that."

"And how would you know?"

"I was a nosy bairn."

"Aye, and I remember just how nosy."

"Please." She ran her thumb along his lower lip. "Kiss me again. Show me your passion."

"You're going to be the end of me." He dipped his head and covered her mouth with his. Lost, and with breathless urgency, he kissed her deeper, darting his tongue over hers until she panted for more. "Annie." He caressed her sides, roamed down and scooped her bottom. Lifting her higher, he made certain she felt every hard inch of him. "This is dangerous."

"Oh." She seized his biceps. "I like your form of danger."

He kissed her again, until their breath mingled as one and the heat between them blazed and swarmed his senses. Damn, he had to stop. Where was his resolve?

Breathing hard, he pulled away. "I hope that will be one kiss you never forget."

"I'm certain of it." She licked her lips and he groaned.

Heaven help him.

He heaved the door open, shut it behind him and adjusted his too-tight trews. Annie was a temptress he had no business playing with. He certainly couldn't allow her to waylay him when his oath to his chief had to come first.

Through the dark weave of passageways, he returned to his chamber and once inside, stripped off his shirt and dunked his head in a basin of icy water. He came up and sent drops flying. Soap in hand, he scrubbed his jaw then ran his dirk across his stubbles.

Dressed in black trews and a leather vest over his tunic, he marched out the door, his mind once again clear.

"Building the bonds between the clans is important." James's voice echoed toward him. "Annie is aware I wish to court her. I would like your permission to do so as well."

Colin stopped outside one of the private rooms where at night men often enjoyed a game or two of cards.

"James, I cannae believe you have the gall to ask such a thing after I was forced to agree to the handfast between her and your brother." Rory's voice. "I dinnae wish her to marry you anymore than I did Alex."

Colin stepped through the doorway. The antechamber's gilt-encrusted walls, carved ceilings and lavishly upholstered furniture gleamed, and at the window overlooking the inner courtyard, Rory stood, his dark blond hair trailing over the tip of a massive claymore holstered to his back, his tunic and breeches damp from training.

James MacDonald palmed the hilt of his sword as he continued, "My brother is happily married, and to a MacLeod no less. All I ask is for some time with Annie, to see if we might make a good match."

"Your request is denied," Colin bit out as he stormed up to James. "I'll never allow you to wed Annie. She deserves far better than the likes of a MacDonald."

James snorted. "Of course you'd say that, but she's been given the choice to decide."

"She'll never choose you. She needs her kin close by and you cannae provide that." He stood side by side with Rory, the MacLeod chief nodding in agreement with him.

"I would never prevent her from visiting Dunvegan," James glanced between them. "As I've already told Rory."

"And what of when she wishes to visit Duart on Mull? She is a MacLean, as much as she is a MacLeod."

"Should she wish to visit the Isle of Mull, I wouldnae stop her."

"The hell you wouldnae." He grasped his sword.

"Colin, remember where you are." Rory laid a restraining hand on his shoulder. "As much as I detest his request, I've still left this choice to Annie. Thankfully, we both know she'll never agree to such a match, so this discussion is moot."

"And if she does agree?" James countered.

"Then I'll convince her otherwise." Rory walked to the door, pulled it wider and gestured for James to leave. "Our conversation is done."

"You believe so, but for peace to prevail, you and I still have much to talk about." James left, but not before sending Colin a look over his shoulder that spoke of a man intent on his mission. The glint of determination in James's eyes was one warning Colin would certainly heed.

"We'll need to keep an eye on him." The hair on Colin's nape stood on end. "He's up to no good."

"Lord Sinclare also spoke to me last eve, although I couldnae find you after he had." Rory scrubbed a hand over his face. "He too put in a formal offer. He needs to take a young wife in the hope of replacing his heir. He lost both his sons last year."

"I'm aware, but Annie has no intention of marrying that man either."

"I agree Sinclare is no' for her. Watch over her for me today. The king has requested my attendance and he willnae accept an apology. I have no choice but to go."

"I too have business to attend to in the city. Arthur will guard her. I've already given him that order, and when I return, I'll watch over her. I'll never allow James MacDonald to court her. On that, I give you my word."

"Rory, there you are." Annie breezed into the room, her full red velvet skirts brushing the floor and her sweet rose scent engulfing Colin. He wanted to drown in that scent. "I hope I'm no' interrupting either of you."

"Nay, never." Rory smiled at her. "Did you sleep well?"

"Very. Will you be around and about this day?"

"No' until this eve. What did you need?"

"I wish to go riding."

"Then take Arthur and Elizabeth as escorts. I'll speak to my captain and ensure he arranges a sufficient guard for the ride. I'm sorry, but I must be away, lass. The king waits for no man." He kissed her cheek and strode out the door.

Annie turned her mischievous gaze on him. "Well, well. We are all alone again, and at a time when I didnae expect to see you."

"Where do you intend to ride?" He crossed his arms in the hope that action would prevent him from reaching for her.

"Around the park." She stepped closer, slid her hands over his crossed arms and dipped her fingers into the gap between. "You look dark and dangerous in full black attire. Would your current business be an activity in which you wish discretion?"

"I'm a warrior. I prefer to wear dark clothing. It aids me in blending into the shadows."

"And you've shaved." She kissed his chin. "Mmm, 'tis so smooth."

"Cease distracting me. This morn, James approached Rory with a request to court you."

"Aye, I've already told you of his wishes." She winked and sashayed out the door.

"Annie." He followed her down the passageway. "Where are you going?"

"To break my fast. If you have time, come and join me."

"I'll make time." His business with Ian could wait a little longer, and he had yet to find Arthur who should have been up and about by now and standing sentry outside her door. He led Annie into the great hall where he found the very man he was after sitting at a trestle table in the far corner. He joined Arthur and scraped a wooden chair out for Annie.

"How are you this day, Arthur?" Annie smiled at Arthur as she sat.

"Very good. Did you sleep well?" He munched on an oatcake.

"Aye, and more soundly than I thought I would." She glanced at Colin as he took the seat next to hers. "I didnae ask. Did you rest well?"

"There was a lump in the bed, one I wasnae used to." A lump with long blond tresses he adored. He hauled out his dirk, cut a slice of bread from the loaf and slathered it in jam before taking a bite.

"Hot oats, sir?" A serving maid appeared with a large tray holding steamy bowls.

He nodded, and she set a bowl before him and Annie.

"That's awful, about the lump, Colin." Annie poured milk over her oats and his, then picked up her spoon. "I cannae stand such things myself. Whenever I find a lump, I roll over it a few times and flatten it out. 'Tis the best way to deal with lumps."

He coughed and almost choked on the bread he munched. "And exactly how often do you find these lumps?"

"More often of late than ever afore." She patted his back. "That's a nasty cough you have. If you like, I could take a look at your lump."

"My lump will be fine."

"If you're sure…"

Arthur scratched his chin. "'Tis been a while since I found a lump in my bed myself."

"Lucky you." Annie giggled. "They can be quite the nuisance and very difficult to get rid of once they make themselves at home."

"Behave." Colin squeezed her leg under the table.

"You started it." She pointed at the bread. "Could you pass me some please?"

"Aye, allow me to feed my lump roller." He cut a slice, added jam and handed it to her.

He enjoyed his meal and the light conversation that followed, no matter that Annie continued with her teasing. Her smile was infectious and lightened his heart. Hell, he'd missed such times like these with her whenever they'd been forced apart.

"Annie." Elizabeth hastened across the great hall and hugged her niece. "Good morn, my dear."

"And good morn to you too."

"Sit here, Elizabeth." He offered her his seat as he stood. "I must be away. Business to attend to in the city. Watch Annie for me. She's in an impetuous mood today."

"She's always in such a mood." Smiling, Elizabeth slid into

his seat. "Travel safely."

"I will." He leaned into Annie's ear and whispered, "Take care as you ride."

"That goes for you too."

He tore himself away from her and crossed to the doors. At the edge of the great hall, he stopped for one last look. 'Twas impossible not to soak in the sight of her. Her smile lit up her face as she spoke to her aunt and Arthur, then she stopped and glanced over her shoulder at him. Her gaze softened and she blew him a kiss.

It hit him square in the chest, like a physical blow that blossomed with heat and spread out to envelope him whole. He was a lost cause.

With that difficult thought consuming him, he left for the stables. He was a captain in his chief's guard, a warrior who went to war when called to do his duty. He couldn't take Annie to wife and expose her to his kind of life. Should he not survive a battle, he'd only bring more heartache down on her head. Aye, she deserved so much more than that.

After saddling his destrier, he rode out the gate and along the cobbled road that ran between Holyrood House and Edinburgh Castle, his heart a heaving mess.

At least there was one thing he knew for certain.

His chief awaited his freedom, and he'd make damn certain 'twas granted.

Chapter 3

Guilt consumed Annie as Colin strode out of the great hall. She'd kept the finer details of her coming excursion with James from both him and Rory and it grated on her. She'd told James she would go riding with him, and she'd keep her word, but she didn't care for the mistruth she'd spoken in order to do so.

"What has that frown on your face, my dear?" Elizabeth swirled honey over her oats and ate a bite.

Voice low so Arthur couldn't overhear, she said, "We're going riding with James MacDonald this morn. I said aye to him last eve when he asked. Colin and Rory know naught about it."

Elizabeth shivered. "We'll have to watch James. Those MacDonalds are a devious bunch."

"This ride is for me to get to know James a little better, only things have changed since he and I spoke." She sipped her tea. "There's a man I'm very interested in, and I dinnae mean James."

"Oh, do tell."

"I'm rather close to him already."

"Hmm, I see." Fluffing her gown's mahogany skirts, Elizabeth's eyes lit. "Now, would that perchance be the strapping young warrior who just left?"

"How did you know?"

"I may have seen how close you two were standing together outside last eve afore I called your name."

"You should have said."

"I thought I did when I asked him so blatantly to dance with you." She propped her elbow on the table and leaned closer. "Some men need a gentle push, and it appears Colin more so than any other. Your mothers were the best of friends and he's always been there to protect you. His dual guardianship of you though may be an issue for Rory. 'Tis no' fitting for him to be courting you when you're his ward."

"Who I wed is my choice. Rory allowed me that decision." That's if Colin could be persuaded to offer for her. He'd kissed her last night and this morning, and the passion simmering between them had flared, although he was still holding back. "I dinnae wish to force his hand and I worry I inadvertently will."

"Colin adores you. If there is force, 'tis of the right nature." Elizabeth squeezed her hand. "I can see the indecision worries you. You should speak to him, and afore 'tis too late."

"What do you mean too late?"

"We both know he's here for more than one reason."

"His chief?"

"Aye, if Rory were in the cells, there isnae a MacLeod warrior who wouldnae be trying to free him."

"What do you think I should do?"

"Follow your heart. That is all any of us can do." She plucked a wedge of cheese from the breadboard and eyeing her, bit into it. "Are you up for the challenge?"

"I am."

"Good. Now no more worrying when we need to ready ourselves for this ride." Elizabeth pushed out her chair and stood. "I do long for some fresh air, even though I must endure James's company while I partake of it."

Why did her kin hate James so much? Aye, they hadn't

spent time with him as she had. Mayhap that was all. He certainly wasn't like his dastardly chief and uncle.

In her chamber, she donned her black riding jacket and boots then emerged from her room to find her aunt in the passageway informing Arthur of the finer details of their ride.

Arthur snorted, clearly not impressed as he eyed her. "I take it Colin isnae aware of what's happening?"

"Nay, but I'll have a guard, and we'll no' be leaving the king's land." She stepped up to him. "Think of this as an enjoyable excursion, naught more."

"I still dinnae care for it."

"James has always been polite and kind to me." She patted Arthur's arm. "Truly, what harm could there be in a short ride in the park when I'll have you there protecting me?"

"Aye, there is little harm with the guard you'll have, and I'd lay my life down for yours." He gripped the hilt of his sword and stroked the gleaming metal.

"I know you would."

He slowly nodded. "We'll go, but you'll follow my every order, and I will be leaving a message here for Colin should he arrive back afore us."

"I'd expect naught less." She'd won the immediate battle. She linked arms with her aunt and together they walked down the passageway and outside into the inner courtyard. At the stables, James and two of his men, along with three of Rory's guard waited with their saddled mounts.

"Annie, good morn." James, with his plaid belted low on his waist and a brown leather vest covering his starched white tunic, caught her hand and dropped a kiss on her knuckles. Dipping his head, he acknowledged her aunt. "Mistress MacLeod, I thought we'd ride through the park afore we enjoy a midday meal at one of the countryside's finest taverns, The King's Tavern."

"That sounds lovely." Elizabeth crossed to her palfrey and a

MacLeod guardsman boosted her into the saddle. She arranged her heavy mahogany skirts around her then grasped the reins.

James steered Annie toward her horse then with his hands on her hips, lifted her up. "Thank you for agreeing to this outing. I know I made it a little difficult to say nay."

"Aye, but I'm looking forward to the ride and being outdoors." How could Colin not see James's true personality? He was nothing like his warring uncle. Certainly ambition drove him, but not in a menacing way.

"We're Highlanders," he said as he mounted his destrier. "We shouldnae be closeted up at court but riding free across our great land."

"Well, of that, I'm in agreement." She slapped the reins against her horse's neck and side-by-side they rode out under the arch with the others following in a steady stream behind. Arthur rode next to her aunt a horse length behind, his gaze a targeted one on James's back. She shook her head at him, but he paid her no mind.

"Dinnae frown so. Your guard simply watches you as he should." James leaned closer. "Although, the MacLeods and MacDonalds have agreed to a truce, even as uneasy as it currently is. I'm just glad MacLean isnae here."

"Colin had other business to attend to, and I also thought it rather prudent no' to tell him."

He chuckled. "Aye, your prudence is much appreciated."

They trotted down the trail, entered the depth of the forest and left the imposing sight of Holyrood House behind. The palace's park, a vast expanse of land stretching for hundreds of acres held glens, lush rolling moors, rocky crags and hidden lochs. 'Twas wonderful to be surrounded by such seclusion mere minutes after leaving the castle.

James too grinned, his shoulders wide as a look of pure pleasure crossed his face. His mop of unruly red curls gave him a youthful look, although the two-handed sword strapped in a baldric across his broad back, stated he was a warrior, born and bred. "Tell me more about yourself, Annie. I'm aware you grew up on Mull afore your father joined the MacLeods at Dunvegan."

"Aye. I was a mischievous bairn, climbing trees and hunting from high in my tree hut." Well, it had been Colin's tree hut, but as he'd grown older and left his youth behind, he'd visited it less often, so she'd claimed it for herself.

"I too had a favorite tree I climbed and hunted from. One day I shall have children and ensure they enjoy such things. Do you desire bairns, Annie?"

"Very much." She yearned to have children, and had since losing her parents. "I will have as many as my husband gives me."

"Then you'll make a wonderful wife, and I only hope mine." A twinkle lit his blue eyes.

"I—" A drop of water splashed her cheek. The skies had darkened overhead, obliterating the clear skies as low cloud rolled in. "The weather changes as fast here as it does in the isles."

"Aye, it does." James glanced toward the hills ahead. "Those storm clouds look particularly heavy that way. Mayhap we'll ride straight to The King's Tavern. An earlier meal willnae hurt us, and I dinnae wish to see you get wet."

"An early lunch sounds wonderful."

He changed their course and veered south-west toward the edge of the park. "You'll like this tavern. I've enjoyed the proprietor's hospitality many a time and the cook makes a hearty stew."

"Then let's race. I feel the need for even more fresh air."

"Aye, what the lady wishes, the lady will have." With a shout, he slapped his mount's flanks with his heels and took off.

Annie raced after him, his exuberance encouraging her own.

* * * *

Dark and ominous clouds gusted in as Colin rode toward his meeting place in the congested heart of Edinburgh. As thunder boomed and lightning slashed, he opened his saddlebags, pulled his heavy black cloak out and slung it over his shoulders before tucking himself lower and picking up his speed.

The heavens opened and rain pounded onto the cobbled road. It streamed downhill, sending the pungent scent of the city from the streets and into the gutters. Along the roadside, two lively children squealed and dashed barefoot into their home while a lanky brown-haired dog chased after them.

At the end of the street, The White Dover Inn with its boarded two-story facade appeared and he pulled up in the courtyard, tossed his reins to a waiting stable hand and dashed indoors.

The inn's crowded main room held a score of patrons seated at small tables, all enjoying a tankard and a meal. Leaving his hood pulled low, he walked toward Ian who sat hunched in the far darkened corner. His man was bereft of his clan plaid, his identity hidden under a hooded cloak as his was.

He slid in beside his man where he'd have a good view of the room. "Is all well?" he asked, keeping his voice low so as not to be overheard.

"Aye, Murdock waits in the forest. We've set up camp in a quiet spot near the park's faerie stones, up on the ridge."

"I know the place. You've had no problem keeping out of sight?" He didn't need the king or his men discovering there were more MacLean warriors in Edinburgh other than himself and Arthur when the possibility of surprise might be needed.

"No one's been able to identify us."

"Good."

A barmaid flounced toward them, a tray of tankards in hand and her bountiful breasts almost spilling from her brown kirtle's low neckline. "What would ye like to quench your thirst, my lovelies?"

"Ale will do, lass."

Raising an appreciative eyebrow, she set a drink before him. "A big man like ye must have a ferocious appetite. Should ye need aught more, holler out."

"I'll no' be hollering, but thank you all the same." The cheeky lass. Colin swatted her bottom and sent her on her way. It had been three long years since he'd last flipped a lass's skirts. Far too long, but he'd yet to meet a lass lately who appealed.

"You never holler, no' since the day you became Annie MacLeod's guardian." Ian took a swig of his ale and eyed the serving girl as she served other patrons at a nearby table. "Is Annie at court as you heard she was?"

"Aye, and seeking a husband."

"You dinnae wish her for yourself?"

"I have a chief to free."

Ian scratched his bristly jaw. "How do the talks between Lachlan and the king go?"

"They've disintegrated. Lachlan now seeks his freedom from the tower, however we can arrange it."

"And he'll have it. What do you need?"

"Lachlan will be waiting for us at midnight on the night of the masquerade." He took a gulp of ale. "I'll meet you and Murdock at the rear of the stables on the morrow's eve. Sneak in amongst the other guests and keep your identities hidden." Suspicion would naturally fall on him and Arthur once they'd escaped with their chief, but there was naught he could do about that, not when his course was now set.

"Will do. The clan will be pleased when we return with our chief."

"Which will also be when the battle truly begins. The king will send his men after us, of that I have no doubt."

"The king needs to leave us be to settle our disputes as we see fit." Ian's words rumbled fierce and low.

Like his men, Colin too detested the king's desire to stamp

his mark of ownership on the isles, to control them as he did the rest of Scotland. "Lachlan will be freed, and very soon." He clapped his man on the back. "We shouldnae linger here for long."

"Aye, Captain. I'll see you the night of the ball." Ian stood and quietly snuck out of the inn, his hood pulled low.

Giving Ian time to ride clear, Colin finished his drink. As he was about to stand, the front door opened and a gust of wind tore in along with two hulking warriors. Both wore the MacDonald plaid, the man at the head none other than Hugh, Donald's nephew and James's cousin. The warrior was hard to miss with his oily black hair plastered to his head and red bulbous nose. Only what was Hugh doing so far from Holyrood when he too awaited word of when he could speak to his captured chief?

Intrigued, Colin tugged his hooded cloak lower and slid deeper into the shadows.

Hugh and his man eased into the screened compartment in front of him. The MacDonalds spoke in hushed tones, though with their deep Erse brogue, he could still make out their conversation.

"The MacLeod chit is out riding with James. I saw her and a contingency of Rory MacLeod's guardsmen leave with my cousin and his men. I dinnae know what James intends, but she's no' for him." Hugh thumped his fist on the tabletop.

"I cannae believe the MacLeod chief has given her the freedom to choose her own husband, but well that works in our favor," the other man answered.

Hell, the men's voices were eerily similar to the two who'd walked past Annie's chamber the night afore and spoken of tracking her in the woods. 'Twas the MacDonalds who schemed and intended to make Annie a pawn in the war between their clans.

The barmaid returned, leaned over Hugh and gave him a lush view of her ample assets. "Can I offer either of ye men some of the inn's fine fare?"

"Aye, you can," Hugh smirked as he grabbed her breasts and squeezed them. "Do you have a chamber, lass? I wish to enjoy in private."

The wench giggled. "Above-stairs, and one all to myself."

Hugh shoved to his feet and followed the maid while his man took a position at the base of the stairs to wait.

Colin tapped his leg. Surely Annie couldn't be out riding with James. Aye, she'd gone riding, but not with his arch enemy, or at least she better not have. He gritted his teeth, slid out of the booth and with his hood still in place, skirted the room and left as discreetly as he could.

If Annie had placed herself in harm's way, he'd lock her in her chamber and throw away the key.

* * * *

The heavens opened and the rain pounded down as Annie rode hard beside James through the forest. The weather had turned fast, but their race to The King's Tavern energized her.

James heaved his horse up before a swollen river and yelled over the whistling wind, "This burn is usually passable here, but with the rain sluicing down from the hills the stream rises fast. Do you still wish to continue on?"

"We're too close to turn back." The rushing water wouldn't stop her. She urged her horse down the bank and plowed through. Waves surged around her palfrey's flanks, but she patted its neck and nudged it up the other side of the bank.

"We seem to have lost the others, but they cannae be too far behind." James joined her, his mount swishing its tail and sending a spray of water flinging through the air.

Behind her, a mist descended and smothered the trees. No sign of their party. "The storm worsens. I cannae see them either, but they know where we're headed and I'm sure they'll follow." Soaked through yet still excited, she grinned. "Come, James. Our race is no' yet done."

"Aye, to The King's Tavern," he bellowed and chuckled.

She spurred her horse on and James rode hard on her heels.

They galloped through the trees another furlong or two then crested a rise. Nestled ahead amongst the towering pine and elm trees, a quaint stone building with smoke puffing from its chimney, beckoned. This would be the perfect spot to enjoy the midday meal.

"You win." James beamed.

"We're no' there yet." She slapped her horse's rear and cantered into the courtyard a mere horse-head in front of him. Giggling, she pulled her mount to a stop and handed the reins to a lad as he rushed out from the stables.

James bounded from his mount, caught her around the waist and swung her down beside him. "'Tis been a long time since I've enjoyed a race quite so much. Let's get inside and out of this rain."

A gust plastered her soggy red velvet skirts against her legs as he steered her toward the tavern's front doors. She patted her wet head, having lost her broad-brimmed hat somewhere back near the river.

The doors opened as they approached and a crinkly-eyed man wearing breeches and a loose plaid over his shoulders waved them in. "Come inside. The wife has mutton stew cooking."

"My thanks." James shook his head and sent drops flying. "The rest of our party follows."

A flush-faced woman with long strands of gray hair trickling free of her bun eased past the man and wiped her hands on the brown apron tied around her ample waist. A stricken look crossed her face as she gazed at Annie. "Oh, my lady. Ye're soaked right through. Come and I'll find ye something dry and warm to wear afore ye eat."

"Thank you. That would be greatly appreciated." She followed the woman inside and up the side stairs leading to the top landing. Doors led off either side of the corridor. She walked past a young maid of perhaps ten and three sweeping the floorboards near the end of the hallway.

"This is my best chamber and 'tis all yours for as long as ye need it. It overlooks the forest." The woman opened the last door and ambled across to a trunk beside a large bed. She pulled out a drying cloth and a clean sark. "Turn around, and I'll help ye unlace your gown. I'm Maud."

"Thank you, Maud. I'm Annie MacLeod. The storm hit so suddenly and I wasnae expecting to arrive here as I did." She unbuttoned her wet riding jacket and with nowhere to put it, set it carefully on the floor.

"Aye, we've had more rain of late and the burn usually overflows its banks when a storm like this passes through."

"My aunt and the rest of our party were right behind us."

"I'll keep an eye out for them."

"Thank you. I'd appreciate that."

Maud tugged her last lacing free, came around in front and helped her shimmy the long clingy velvet and lace-edged sleeves down her arms.

With her gown in a puddle at her feet, she shivered.

Maud wrapped her in the drying cloth and rubbed her chilled flesh. "We'll have ye warm in no time. Was that ye husband below?"

"Nay, 'twas—" Heat flushed her cheeks. Goodness. She was alone, albeit by chance. "Maud, I need to ask a favor. I'm cousin to the Chief of MacLeod, and I need a chaperone until my aunt arrives. Do you know of anyone who might aid me?"

"Aye, my daughter should be suitable." She opened the door and called out to the girl with the broom. "Milly, fetch the blue gown from the trunk in my chamber and matching slippers. Hurry, lass. Ye've an important job to do." Maud returned and held out the dry sark.

Annie lifted her arms and sighed as the white linen fluttered over her head and swamped her in a layer of warmth. The girl with long brown hair and doe-like eyes dashed inside and passed her mother a gown.

"Milly, meet Mistress MacLeod. Ye're to be her maid while she's with us. Whatever she asks, ye are to do."

She dipped her head.

Annie smiled at the lass. "Nice to meet you, Milly. Could you help me with those slippers?"

"Aye, my lady." She knelt and eased them onto her feet while Maud laced Annie's gown.

"That's so much better. My thanks to you both."

"Ye're welcome. Take a seat and I'll tidy your hair." Maud picked up a brush from the side table. "Milly, take Mistress MacLeod's clothing downstairs. I'll wash the garments after I've served the midday meal and then return and dry them afore this fire. Bring a mop, and some peat for the fire too."

"Aye, Mother." The girl scooped up the wet clothes and hurried out the door.

"She's a bright lass that one, and has quite the baker's hand." Maud smiled proudly as she separated each section of Annie's hair. Mindful of the tangles, she took care as she brushed out the wet length.

Before long, Milly returned and set to work building the fire. She lit and stoked it into life. Heat pulsed into the room and warmed Annie through. If only her aunt were here enjoying this warmth with her. Elizabeth was an accomplished rider and adored the outdoors as she did. She should be here soon. Worry gnawed at her.

"All done and dry." Maud set the brush down and eyed her daughter. "Ye're to remain with Mistress MacLeod while she's here. No running off to attend to other tasks unless she asks it of ye."

The lass nodded as she rose from the hearth.

Annie walked out the door and downstairs, eager to see if

her aunt had arrived. With Milly one step behind, she hurried into the main room. Each table was separated from the other by wooden screens. Warriors, farmers, and travelers enjoyed the stew and tankards of ale while they chatted. Her aunt wasn't among them, or any from her party. She slowed next to the fireplace nestled against the wall and rubbed her hands as the rain outside pelted the narrow windows overlooking the courtyard. No sign of any new arrivals out there either.

"Annie." James rose from one of the screened tables attired in borrowed clothes. The black tunic and trews were too dark on him, but the red, blue and green plaid tossed over his shoulders lessened the austere look. A worried look creased his brow. "Are you warm enough?"

"I am now, thank you." She sat in the booth while Milly took a seat near the wall, not close enough to overhear their conversation, but in the perfect spot to keep a good watch. "I need someone to ride back to the river and search for my aunt. She'll be so anxious."

"The tavern owner informed me when the river becomes impassable, one has to track higher into the hills and hope for a spot where it isnae too swollen to cross. I've already sent the stable lad down to the river to check. Dinnae fear, Annie. We'll make the best of this situation and be none the worse for it." He crossed his arms along the table and leaned closer. "If you'd like me to arrange aught more, then you need only—" He coughed and thumped his chest. "You need only—" He coughed again.

"Are you all right?"

"'Tis a tickle in my throat, no more."

Maud ambled across and slid a tray onto the planked table. She set a bowl of stew before them both, each dish holding a thick slice of bread wedged half into it.

"That looks wonderful, Maud. Thank you." She breathed in the mouth-watering scent of mutton and vegetables. "Could you save some for my aunt, please."

"Of course." Maud sauntered to the next table.

Annie scooped up the bread, took a big bite and licked the richly flavored juices as they dribbled from the end. Hearty and delicious.

"Is it good?" James picked up his spoon and dipped it into his stew.

"Wonderful."

He sneezed and set his spoon down.

"Are you sure you're well, James?"

"Well enough." A gust of wind blew in and the stable lad hurried across and stopped before them. James stood and asked the lad, "Did you find any sign of our party having crossed the river?"

"The tracks on the other side of the river gave proof half the riders headed uphill, while the other half, appeared to have returned to Holyrood."

"Is it possible for us to leave?" She rose to her feet as she questioned the lad. She couldn't remain here when her aunt would worry so.

He shook his head. "There's no way through."

"All will be well, Annie. Your aunt has a strong guard." James handed the lad a coin and thanked him. "The riders must have separated in order to find a way to pass."

"Aye." What more could she do? She would have to wait out this storm. She scrunched her chilled hands in her skirts and sent a prayer heavenward for her aunt's safe return to Holyrood.

* * * *

Colin paced Elizabeth's chamber as she huddled before the fire swaddled in a thick fur after riding into Holyrood House drenched from her ride. He'd returned mere minutes before her and been given the message Arthur had left him. Annie rode with MacDonald. Never had such anger, frustration and concern raged through him.

He knelt at Elizabeth's feet and grasped her hands. "Are

you certain Annie crossed the river without issue?"

"Her tracks led up the embankment on the other side and away, as did James's. Rory's guardsmen even searched downstream during our return to be certain all was as we believed. I dinnae know how they got so far ahead of us, but they crossed the river afore the storm waters rose and breached the river's banks. We could find no way to cross."

"You said Arthur continued up into the hills in search of a passable point."

"As well as two of James's men and one of Rory's guards. I'm no' sure know how long it'll take them to reach her, and now 'tis so dark outside."

"Did the guardsmen who returned with you ride back out again?"

"They did, immediately."

"Then I'll try to catch them up and find her." Rain slashed the window and a chilly blast of air whistled down the chimney and sent the embers flaring. He tossed another log onto the fire and strode to the door.

"Colin, wait. She does no' love him." Tears pooled in Elizabeth's eyes. "Dinnae let MacDonald find a way to take her away from us. I fear that will happen with them being left alone."

"I'll find her and bring her home. Let Rory know I've left but will return with her afore dawn. No one will take her from me. Of that I can assure you." He stormed from her chamber, gathered his satchel and all he needed for the ride and galloped out the gates.

Riding hard, he urged his destrier through the forest, keeping as close as he could the river's winding path. The storm waters surged over its sides, a murky black in the dark abyss of the night. As the rain beat down on him, his thoughts plagued him. Annie thrived on the outdoors, would take any challenge and dare another to join her.

Throughout his life, she'd issued challenges to him countless times. The first had been not long after he'd built his tree hut. She'd insisted she could take down the first small creature with her bow, so side-by-side they'd sat on the front platform of his hut high in the treetops, his long legs swinging over the edge next to her tiny feet.

He'd spotted the half-hidden rabbit in the brush first, released his arrow and taken down his prey. Annie had squealed her delight for his win, and from that day forth, she'd issued challenge after challenge in the hope of beating him.

Thunder rumbled across the night sky and lightning hit the tree behind him with a sizzling crackle. His mount reared on its hind legs then crashed down and bolted into the river. The waters swirled and surged around him. He shoved his knees into his destrier's flanks and forced the animal to swim with the flow rather than risk going against the turbulent current. The white-capped rapids carried them downstream and at the river bend, he jerked on the reins, caught leverage on the stony bed and with a heave and splash, slogged to the other side. Colin roared his victory as he made solid ground.

Now to rescue Annie.

Riding hard, he tore down the trail toward The King's Tavern, galloped into the courtyard and woke a groggy-eyed stable lad. "I've come from Holyrood House in search of Mistress MacLeod. I'm her guardian, Colin MacLean. Can you tell me where she is?"

"Aye, ye're the first from the traveling party to arrive. She's upstairs, the last chamber at the end of the passageway. My sister, Milly, remains with her as her chaperone."

Good. Annie had been wise to ensure such a thing.

"Is there a way inside without waking the proprietors?" He'd rather get Annie clear of here before he confronted James. MacDonald could wait, whereas Annie and her reputation couldn't. Sneaking her out and returning her to Holyrood before the castle awoke was imperative. Aye, the less who knew what had happened this day, the better.

"Ye can use the back door near the kitchen." The lad lugged a key from his breeches pocket and handed it across.

"I'll return soon, and should my man, Arthur MacLean, or any of her MacLeod guardsmen arrive in that time, tell them to wait for me."

"Aye, sir."

"If you've time, give my horse some oats and rub him dry." He paid the lad, used the key and slunk inside the inn.

Water dripped and pooled at his feet as he snuck across the kitchen and around the center wooden bench piled high with cleaned pots. He ducked under the low doorframe and keeping to the shadows, whisked up the side stairwell to the landing. All was quiet above-stairs, each door leading off the darkened corridor firmly shut. He stopped at the last door, turned the knob and crept inside. A fire burned low in the hearth, the glowing embers lighting his way. He eased around a pallet on the floor where a lass with tangled brown tresses slept, then without making a noise, knelt at the side of the large bed.

Annie slept, her long white-blond hair a silky halo tumbling over her pillow. He lifted a lock and ran it through his fingers. "I've missed you, scamp."

"Mmm," she murmured as she rolled onto her side and curled her cheek into her palm. She was such an innocent, but his innocent.

"Annie, love," he whispered as he gently pressed his hand over her mouth. He didn't care to startle her, but he couldn't take the risk of waking the child and causing a stir. 'Twas best no one knew he'd come until they were well gone. "'Tis I, Colin."

Annie's lashes drifted open and her eyes lit with happiness. Slowly, she glided her hand over his and plucked his fingers away. "I'm awake, and very glad to see you. Have you seen my aunt?"

"She's well, and resting at Holyrood. You though, are in a world of trouble." He leaned in and kissed her, and not nearly as long and deeply as he wished to.

"When am I not?" She swept her hands around his neck, dragged him down and with her heart beating against his, kissed him as if she'd feared never to see him again.

One taste was all it took to cloud his senses. He urged her lips apart and plundered the sweet depths of her mouth until her tongue tangled with his in a heated duel.

"Thank you for coming for me," she whispered against his lips.

"I will always come for you, although you're never to go riding with MacDonald again and we shall have stern words about this upon our return." He pulled back an inch, one difficult inch, but thankfully 'twas all he needed to gather some control. "I discovered who the other two men scheming against you are. They're MacDonalds as well. Scourges, the lot of them."

"The MacDonalds are always scheming against our clan, but no' James." She sat and pushed the covers off. "He wishes for peace. He truly does, Colin."

"You're defending him? Even now after he took you away from me?" How could she trust the man so implicitly?

"He never took me away. If aught, 'tis my fault we lost the rest of our party. I challenged James to a race and we rode through the river before the storm waters rose."

"Such a thing will never happen again." He took her hand and helped her up. "Come, we must be away."

She tiptoed across the wooden floorboards to the clothes-rack where her clothes dried before the fire. She slid her red velvet gown over her head and wriggled it down.

He stepped in behind her and laced the stays then helped her don her riding jacket and boots. "Ready?"

"Aye."

Holding her hand and following the exact route he'd taken

in, he led the way out the door and downstairs through the dark. Outside, he stopped and Annie bumped into him from behind.

"What are we waiting for?" She squeezed his fingers.

Across the night-shrouded courtyard, all remained eerily still.

"Stay close." He withdrew his sword. "All is too quiet."

Chapter 4

Annie and Colin had to leave without causing a stir or waking a soul. Pulse pounding, she tiptoed in Colin's footsteps as he skirted the edge of the inner courtyard alongside the wooden outbuildings. He kept to the shadows, stopping every few steps to ensure she remained close behind.

Near the entrance to the stables, he pressed her against the wall. "Stay," he hushed. "Since I found a way across the river, the others might have as well. I dinnae care right now to deal with any MacDonalds."

"Be careful." 'Twas her fault he was here.

"Always." With his claymore raised, he snuck inside.

Eyes squeezed shut, she clung to the wall. A shuffle and a slap ricocheted toward her then nothing.

"Arthur is here." Colin appeared out the dark.

She gasped and grabbed his shirtfront. "What about the others?"

"Arthur crossed upstream, although he barely made it through. The others willnae be far behind him." Arms wrapped around her, he kissed her forehead and murmured in her ear, "We must leave, as quick as we can."

"Then why are we still standing here?"

"Because Arthur is bringing the horses out and I was rather enjoying this stolen moment." The moonlight tracking through a break in the dark clouds above lit his golden gaze.

"You're a terrible tease, and you should be more concerned about your own safety." She pushed past him and marched into the stables.

Frowning, Arthur led her palfrey toward her. Water dripped from his wet hair onto his deerskin cloaked shoulders. "You are a troublesome lass, Annie MacLeod."

"Aye, I'm sorry you've been riding all night to reach me."

"The others will find a stretch of the burn to cross soon, just as I did." He eyed Colin who stepped in behind her. "Although I would like to know how you managed to arrive afore me."

"My horse apparently has wings." Colin caught her around the waist and lifted her into her saddle. He fixed her skirts, collected his destrier from Arthur and mounted. "We'll ride right through. No stopping."

Arthur nudged his horse into the clear night air and rode out.

Colin glanced at her. "Do I need to issue a challenge?"

"Nay, but I will. Race you." Energized again, she flew through the night.

Colin pounded in beside her, his dark hair whipping about his shoulders and his watchful gaze alert on their surroundings.

As they reached the river's edge where she'd first managed to cross, Arthur slowed and jumped down. Assessing the water's depth, he wandered along the bank then returned and leapt into his saddle. "This is now passable. I'll go first."

He urged his horse through the muddy waters flowing with debris and up the other side before waving out for her to follow.

She bundled her skirts higher, showing a few inches of leg but better that than get sopping wet again. Colin groaned and she raised a brow. "Is there a problem?"

"Aye, you, and you're a mighty one at that." He slapped her

palfrey's flanks and her horse jerked forward and splashed into the river. Halfway across, a tumbling log riding the waves caught on a protruding rock and bounced off. It skimmed past her mount's front legs with barely an inch to spare before crashing into the bank.

"Move on, quick," Colin ordered as he came closer.

She nudged her horse, climbed the verge and joined Arthur.

"Next stop, Holyrood House." Arthur tapped his heels to his horse's sides and rode into the dark.

"Come here, trouble." Colin leaned across, caught her hand and kissed her knuckles.

"That's scamp to you." She slapped her reins on her horse's neck and lying low, followed in Arthur's tracks through the forest.

Never had she felt so safe, regardless of their mad dash through the night.

Throughout her life, Colin had always been there, and she didn't want to know a day when he wouldn't be. Aye, she wanted him in her bed and holding her each night as he had at Holyrood. Hopefully, he wished for the same.

As the night sky lightened, they left the forest behind and galloped toward the palace with its ever-watchful guardsmen patrolling the barbican.

"'Tis almost dawn." She rubbed her cold nose.

"Aye, but we've made it back in time." Colin sent her a reassuring look as they drew up before the stables. He jumped from his mount, slung his satchel over his shoulder and swung her down beside him. "You look cold. Time for a warm bed and plenty of rest."

"Aye, please. I've had enough riding for the day, although I need to see Elizabeth first." Exhaustion seeped into every muscle and she swayed against him as they walked inside. They snuck through the side entrance near the service quarters and once at her aunt's door, she knocked. "Aunt Elizabeth, 'tis Annie."

The door flew open with a whoosh. "Oh, my dear. Thank goodness Colin found you." Her aunt squeezed her tight, her soft lavender scent floating around her. Over her shoulder, she said to Colin, "Thank you. I knew you'd return with her as you promised."

"Aye, and now I'll remain in her chamber, guarding her with my life while she sleeps."

"Good. I dinnae know if my poor heart could take anymore." Elizabeth rubbed her thumbs under Annie's eyes. "Go and rest so these dark circles will be gone for this eve's ball. I'll let Rory know of your return."

"Is he very upset?"

"He knew Colin would find you."

"I'm sorry I caused you any concern." She hugged her again.

"You're back, safe and well, and that's all that matters. Rest well."

"Good night." She trudged into her chamber, Colin her ever-present shadow.

He bolted the door and built a fire to roaring life, although his damp clothes clung to him.

"Let me help you." Yawning, she leaned over him from behind, her white-blond hair sliding forward around his face as she freed the front of his padded leather cotun. Carefully, she eased it off his shoulders and hung it over the chair next to the fire.

"I'm used to the elements. Being a little wet will never hurt me." He added another log, rose to his feet and faced her. "Ready yourself for bed."

"After I've seen to you." She loosened the top laces of his tunic, gripped the hem and lifted his clammy shirt over his head. His wide chest held a smattering of hair, the same dark shade as his head, and his arms and shoulders were hard and packed with muscle. So beautiful, if one could call a hardened warrior that.

Her tiredness fluttered away and unable to help herself, she trailed a finger over his contoured abs and down to the waistband of his leather trews.

"Annie." He groaned and shook his head. "I can undress myself."

"I'm sure you can, but you're wet because of me." She swished to the side table and grabbed a drying cloth. Carefully, she rubbed the remaining moisture from his chest and arms then sashayed around him and stroked his shoulders and back. Muscles flexed and rippled, everywhere. Nay, not just beautiful, but glorious.

"You have to cease." He caught her hand and tugged her around to face him. "You're killing me."

She flicked him with the cloth. "Death by a drying cloth? I think no'."

"You know what I mean. I have very little willpower when it comes to you."

"Nay, you have far too much willpower."

"I want to kiss you, and I'd prefer no' to stop." He slid his hand under her hair and around her nape, his fingers firm and warm on her skin. "Except that'll only lead to danger."

"You always meet danger head on. Dinnae stop now."

"I'm running out of time."

"Because you intend to rescue your chief?"

"Aye, this coming eve, the night of the masquerade. I'll be gone soon after, and unable to protect you."

Unable to court her either. Pain lanced through her. His intentions were clear. He was leaving, and soon. His duty to his chief and clan came first, something she adored and would never halt him from.

Shakily, she stepped back. "All will be well. I have Rory so you must no' worry. I'll take the utmost care while you're gone."

"Where are you going?"

"I'll never stop you from doing your duty. I understand."

He caught her hand and halted her retreat. "You cannae accept another man's proposal while I'm gone."

"Rory isnae leaving until I've secured an engagement. Even should you still wish to aid me in selecting the right man, you'll be gone for weeks. I dinnae have weeks, no' if I wish to decide my own path and ensure the king cannae demand another match."

"That's no' what I meant."

"I'll no' speak of your intention to rescue your chief. It comes as no surprise to me that you had a plan to do so."

"You still misunderstand. I cannae leave you knowing James MacDonald waits in the wings. There is only one thing for it." He hauled open his satchel, tugged his plaid out and tore a short strip from it. He clasped his right hand with her right and wrapped the plaid around both their wrists. The symbolic gesture had her pulse racing. "Annie, I wish a handfast. Bind yourself to me as my wife for a year and a day, and afore that time has passed, I'll ensure we're wed proper."

"Pardon?"

"You cannae marry James."

"And you cannae ask me to marry you because you feel a sense of duty toward me." She shook her head. "Nay, I—"

"I love you, Annie. There is no sense of duty in the deep desire I have for you."

"What did you just say?" Her heart fluttered with hope.

"I love you, and as much as I wish to protect you from enduring a life with me, I'm too selfish to let you go." He lowered to his knees, brought their joined hands to his lips and kissed her palm. "Speak vows with me. I'll begin." He cleared his throat. "I, Colin Eoin MacLean, of Mull, pledge my troth to Annie MacLeod. With this handfast, I take her as my wife for the next year and a day." He tightened his grip on her hand. "I want you as mine, in every single way."

"As I want you. I cannae believe this is happening." She

sank to the floor, her fingers twined with his. "I, Annie MacLeod, of Skye, pledge my troth to Colin Eoin MacLean. With this handfast, I take him as my husband for the next year and a day. Now what do we do?"

"We seal the vows with a kiss." Gaze smoldering, he dipped a finger down her neck and along her riding jacket's square-cut neckline. "Come closer."

She swayed forward and he captured her lips in a scorching kiss, his hard body a fierce heat that stamped warmth into hers just as she desired.

"My wife," he murmured against her lips. "As you always should have been." He rose to his feet and drew her up, untied the plaid binding them and removed her jacket. With his hands on her shoulders, he turned her around and unlaced her gown. He smoothed the red velvet down over her sark until it fell in a swish to her ankles. "Time for bed."

"I need to wash up. I'm grubby from my ride."

"Then make it quick."

She crossed to the water basin, unfolded a cloth and dipped it. With her foot braced on the wooden chair, she lifted the hem of her sark, draped it over her bent knee and cleaned her ankles of the mud splatters from the trail.

"There's something I need to speak of." Colin sat in the chair, took the cloth from her and propped her foot in his lap. Gently, he wiped around her calf and over her knee as he tracked upward. His warm breath whispered across her flesh then puffed hotly along her inner thigh.

Toes curled into his soft leather trews, she held his shoulder. "I'm listening."

"With my coming mission being a dangerous one, I need to know you're safe. You are to return to Dunvegan with Rory. I'll come for you there, as soon as I'm able." His golden gaze lifted to hers, so hungry and needy. "I also cannae take the risk of getting you with child, but if you wish, I would still love to give you pleasure this night." He lowered her leg, lifted the other and stroked higher, until the thin white cotton bunched across her most private parts. "Your pleasure will bring me pleasure."

"If it involves more of this kind of touching, then aye."

"I promise it will." He caught her around the waist and pulled her across his lap.

Straddling him, she wrapped her arms around his neck. "I trust you."

"Dinnae let go." He eased her hem higher and pressed the cool cloth against her entrance. A pulse skittered to life where he touched her and she rocked forward with a low moan. 'Twas past time for them to deepen their bond.

"I want your hands on me, and mine on you." She caressed his glorious chest. "Everywhere."

"Aye, everywhere." He tossed the cloth onto the side table and slowly removed her sark, one inch at a time until she sat naked before him. With his finger, he traced around her beading nipples. "You're so beautiful."

"Oh, everywhere is good."

"Tell me if I go too fast." He clamped her bottom and kept her tight against him as he sucked her nipple deep into his mouth.

She leaned into him, desperate to rub against the hard length of his erection thrusting upward and tenting his trews. "It seems I like fast."

"Delicious," he moaned and drew the tip deeper.

Wicked tingles raced through her body, but needing to touch him too, she tip-toed her fingers down his chest and toward the trail of hair disappearing below his waistband. "Can I do to you as you're doing to me?"

"Later. I want to touch and taste all of you first." He lifted and carried her to the bed, his need burning in his gaze. Carefully, he slid her onto the soft brown fur, eased her breasts together and dipped his head. The raspy stroke of his tongue across the sensitive tips sent a bolt of pleasure to her core.

"You're over dressed, Colin." She fumbled with the ties of his trews. "Take these off."

He eased onto his elbows, gripped the loosened waistband and shoved the leather down his thickly muscled legs and off. His cock bobbed free and brushed his belly, one very large cock with a plump head darkening to a delectable plum color. Sweet heaven, 'twas just as well he wasn't intending to consummate their vows after all. Surely he must fit inside her, except she wasn't exactly certain how.

"What are you thinking, feeling?" He knelt between her legs and his balls drew tighter and higher into the thatch of dark brown curls covering the apex of his groin.

"I'm no' nervous, but there's something else." She squirmed back to make more room for him.

"Nay, stay." He caught one ankle, dragged her back down and feasted his gaze on her below. "If it's fear you have, then when the time comes, I'll fit inside you, right where I belong."

"I may fear but I also want, desperately." She squeezed her eyes shut as a myriad of emotions tumbled through her. This was the moment she'd been waiting a lifetime for and she didn't want to miss a moment of it.

"Look at me, Annie."

She opened her eyes.

"Touch me if you wish. I need to feel your hands on me."

Aye, that's what she needed to. She ran her thumb across his warm lips. His body was all hard angles and heat, and she adored it all, but his soft mouth drew her. Dizzy, and a little breathless, she murmured, "I love you."

"As I love you. I'm sorry it took me so long to tell you exactly how much." He lifted her right foot, massaged her calf then trailed upward, kneading with delicious strokes to her knee before he set her foot down and did the same with the other. "I want you to relax. Elbows down and rest back."

She laid her head on the pillow, her trust in him absolute.

He raised her legs and hooked them over his shoulders until her bottom lifted off the bed and she lay fully exposed to him. "You're beautiful, so pink and lush."

"I'm also yours."

"Aye, mine." Grinning, he swept his hands up her inner thighs, parted her folds and plunged one finger deep inside her. She bucked as pleasure ricocheted outward from her core and hardened her nipples further. "I see you like that."

"I have a feeling I'll like everything you do."

He stroked her harder, faster, rubbing his thumb across her nub until she arched into his touch. "Are you ready for more?"

"Aye," she panted, "but more of what?"

"'Tis best I show you." He added a second finger then dipped his head. Surely he wasn't going to—

He licked her flesh in the most intimate way then thrust both fingers in. Such exquisite torture, and such a deep and delicious rhythm. Every flick of his tongue and stroke of his fingers had her striving for something beyond her reach. Whatever it was, the sensations kept building, higher and higher.

"Colin." Before she lost her mind, she searched and skimmed the hard length of his cock. She caressed his hot flesh and instinct took over. She pumped him in time with how he stroked her until he moaned, long and low. Although she needed more, to have his mouth on hers, to have the glorious length of his body pressing down on every inch of her. "Please, kiss me."

He lifted up, took her mouth in a hot kiss even as he continued to stroke his fingers into her so perfectly below.

She wanted to let go, take whatever beckoned so close and claim it, but not without him. Stroking him harder, she teetered on the verge of a precipice she wanted to fly from.

"I cannae hold on, Annie." He flicked her clit and she tumbled over the edge and soared. Her core rippled with wave after wave of pure bliss and a bright rainbow of colors burst behind her closed eyelids in the most stunning display.

Colin roared, his seed spurting across the bed sheet, his own release coming hard on the heels of hers.

* * * *

Sensations had stormed through Colin as Annie had come around his fingers. She'd taken his cock in hand and given him unexplainable pleasure, just as she'd done with her responsive body. And when she'd come, his own release had pounded through him. He'd shuddered in her hand and followed her over into the poignant abyss of no return.

He slumped on top of her, completely spent.

"Nay, dinnae sleep." She caught his face between her hands and pulled his mouth back to hers. Her kiss, so sweetly seductive, stirred his shaft back to life. "I've never felt the like afore. 'Twas magical, as if you took me to another realm."

"I was no' sleeping, just resting."

"Rest is for later." She kissed him again and he kissed her back. She was so alluring with her beautiful creamy skin and luscious pouty lips. It had been almost impossible not to lose all control and bury himself deep inside her.

"You are going to be the end of me."

"I hope so." She pushed him onto his back and crawled on top of him. Every inch of her glorious body was on stunning display as she sat across his hips and stretched her arms high above her head. As she wriggled against his groin, rubbing her slit over the base of his cock wedged between them, her breasts swayed, heavy and full and demanding his attention. "Oh, this feels so nice."

"Aye, and you're giving me wicked thoughts." Slowly, he grazed a finger from between her breasts to her belly, and as her breathing quickened, he trailed lower.

She glanced at his hand and smiled. "I tingle below."

"You may be too sensitive for my touch. Tell me if you are." He swirled through the pale blond curls covering her entrance and rubbed her nub.

Gasping, she squirmed back. "Aye, too sensitive. Mayhap, I might have a turn to love you the way you just loved me." On her belly between his legs, her breasts falling softly either side of his balls, she slid her hand around his cock.

Oh hell. If she took him in her mouth, he'd lose it.

Peeking through her long lashes, she raised a brow. "I take it I can do this since you put your mouth on me?"

"Aye, but it isnae a good idea."

"Why?" She dipped her head, and in one long teasing stroke, licked him from root to tip.

He groaned. "I'm sensitive too."

"Too bad. I need to touch you." She cupped his balls and caressed them, then with a grin, settled her lips over his head and took him deep.

"Annie." He lifted his hips, his cock hardening impossibly further as her sweet mouth seared him. Such torture, yet he couldn't for the life of him stop her. He cradled her head in his hands and held on as she bobbed up and down. "You learn too fast."

"I have a good teacher, and you are delicious too. I had no idea." She sucked harder and he pushed deeper inside her mouth. He got lost as a sexual haze consumed him. Nay, he needed to remain in control and he certainly couldn't come before he'd seen to her pleasure again first. She needed to experience all he could give her, no matter the short amount of time they had left.

Hands on her waist, he lifted her up onto her knees, scooted down on his back on the mattress and planted his head between her thighs. Underneath her, he tapped her bottom. "Open wider for me."

She gasped but widened her legs. "I wasnae done."

"Too bad." Hmm, where did he start? Her inner flesh, lit by the glow of the flickering flames, sent a golden wash over the pink. And that tiny nub lay temptingly plump and awaiting his touch. "I need to get my fill of you. Brace yourself, scamp."

Blood pounding, he took her clit between his lips and sucked. He lavished attention on her until she moaned and rocked her hips then ground down on him.

"I feel too hot."

"Just how I want you." He reached up and tweaked her nipples, the tips so incredibly hard and pointy. He needed a taste of those too. He flipped her onto her back, rose overtop and adored every lush inch of her breasts.

"Colin, too much, too much," she murmured, her back arching as she pressed those sweet morsels even deeper into his mouth.

"Or no' enough." He teased his teeth over each sensitive tip then swirled with his tongue until fire raced through his blood.

"I cannae hold on."

Neither could he. His cock was hammering at him for release as it jabbed the inside of her thigh. So close. An inch to the right and he'd graze her hot flesh. Nay, he had to think about the days ahead and his promise to her.

He moved away, pressed his cock hard into the soft hollow near her hip and stroked a finger through her heat. She bucked against him and his balls tightened, his cock twitching. She was so wet and he wanted.

"Colin." She cried out his name as she thrashed underneath him, then she came, her inner muscles clamping down and dragging his fingers in.

"You're mine, always mine," he growled as he came in a hot rush.

"Aye, as you're mine," she murmured, her eyelids drifting down.

Chapter 5

Curled on her side, her bottom snug in the curve of Colin's groin, Annie woke more content and rested than she ever had before. She wriggled around and squinted as the late afternoon sunshine streamed through the wooden shutters over her narrow window.

With a hand shielding the glare, she smiled at her new husband who still slept so soundly. A beam of sunlight played over the wispy blond ends of his brown shoulder-length hair and across his high cheeks. His chin, sharply defined with a deep cleft in the center, held such rugged appeal. She kissed the delectable indent then nibbled along his bottom lip. His breathing changed, and even though he showed no other outward sign of having awoken, he clearly had.

"Do you intend to sleep the day away?" she teased him.

"I'm enjoying your touch too much." He opened his eyes and his molten gold gaze melted her.

"You are a temptation beyond aught I've ever known." She hooked one leg over his and pressed her breasts against his chest. The fine dark hairs tickled her nipples and made them stiffen. "Take me with you when you leave with Lachlan. You know I can ride fast."

"Nay, if you got hurt, it would kill me." He wrapped his arms tightly around her. "Naught has ever felt so right holding you, loving you, but the day is disappearing and I must ensure I have all that is needed in place for this eve. Arthur will be wondering where I am."

"Then you must go." She hated the thought of letting him leave, but she couldn't hold him back from his preparations, not when his life could very well depend on it. She rolled away, rested her back against the headboard and pulled the bed sheet up. "Will I see you at the masquerade?"

"Of course you will." He shuffled out, dressed and strapped on his weapons.

"What will you be wearing?" She'd had a gown specifically made for the ball, one a little too risqué, but nevertheless perfect for the masque.

"I procured a monk's habit afore I arrived." He slid his hand underneath the sheet and caressed her leg. "I want you to enjoy yourself this eve, and no' to worry about me."

"I will worry, but I also have faith you'll succeed in your mission."

"Aye, I have you to come back to and that knowledge will spur me on." His fingers skated higher then he groaned and stepped back.

"Could you find me a clean sark so I too can dress?" She lifted her arms and the sheet slithered to her lap.

He glanced away, raked a hand through his hair and strode to her trunk. With her undergarment shielding his gaze, he returned and slid it over her head. "You're a vixen."

"Aye, but your vixen."

He perched next to her on the bed and pulled his boots on.

"Promise me you willnae take any unnecessary risks." She crawled in behind him and massaged his shoulders.

"I give you my word." He pressed back against her. "Lachlan will be freed, then Arthur and I and the two men who'll be joining us will ride hard and fast for the Isle of Mull. Once all is calm, I'll come for you." He caught her hands, brought them around his neck and kissed her palms.

"Once you're gone, I'll have to tell Rory of our handfast," she whispered in his ear. "I'll have no choice."

"'Tis my responsibility to tell him." He caught her around the hips, swept her onto his lap and took her mouth in a slow and tender kiss. "I wish I'd claimed you three years ago."

"I wish you had too."

"I love you, Annie. Never doubt that." He stood, set her on her feet and slung his satchel over his shoulder. "Bar the door." He slipped outside and took a piece of her heart with him as he did.

"I love you too," she breathed into the still chamber, her heart an aching mess as she slid the bolt home. "And I want a lifetime with you."

* * * *

Colin's gut gnawed in the most vicious way as he strode down the passageway toward his chamber. 'Twas pure torture leaving Annie, as was the thought he might have missed his chance with her. Unbelievably, he had James MacDonald to thank for spurring him to action.

"Captain." Arthur caught him up as he walked into his room. "I've just returned from the city." He closed the door, dropped his traveling bag on the end of Colin's bed, flipped the top leather flap and pulled out a black hooded robe and plain white mask with eye cutouts. "I realize you intended to dress as a monk, but I spoke to a merchant and discovered many of the men attending this eve would be wearing garb such as this. I procured three identical costumes, one for you, myself, and Lachlan. The dark fabric will shield our identities when we take the tower, as well as when we ride out."

"Good thinking. Leave a robe and mask for me. I've no problem wearing that instead."

"I also visited a healer and purchased a vial of sleeping potion. She insisted 'twas very potent. One drop in a man's ale will send him to sleep for an hour." Arthur removed it from his pocket and passed the vial across. "I'll spike the ale and have it delivered to them."

"Aye, there are few men who'd turn down a celebratory drink." He handed it back. "Ian and Murdock will meet us at midnight at the rear of the stables. I'll collect them while you see to the ale."

A knock sounded and he opened the door.

Annie's maid stood with a tray in her hands. "Mistress MacLeod requested I bring a meal to you."

"Then give her my thanks." He motioned for the lass to set the steaming bowl of stew and the trencher of meat on the side table. "I have a request in return. I need a single white rose delivered to your mistress. Tell her 'tis a gift from me." Every time he'd sailed from Duart to Dunvegan, he'd always taken her a rose from one of the wild copses she and her mother had planted along the forest trail near their home. She adored white roses.

"There are some bushes with late blooms in the garden. I shall fetch one and take it to her immediately." She bobbed her head and closed the door behind her as she left.

Arthur chuckled. "'Tis grand to see you so smitten."

"I only wish I could court Annie proper. Instead I'm leaving her when 'tis the last thing I wish to do." He stripped off his tunic in favor for a good luck charm. He donned his darkest shirt of coal black with exquisite embroidery around the cuffs and neckline. Annie had made it and stitched it herself, a gift for his last birthday. He touched the fine sapphire-colored thread she'd sewn in a swirling Celtic design around a tiny symbol of a castle tower and the words *Virtue Mine Honor*, his clan's motto. "Annie and I spoke handfast vows this morn."

Arthur grinned. "Well, about damn time. Good to see you

came to your senses."

"Once we've returned to Duart with Lachlan and all has settled, I'll sail for Dunvegan and collect her."

Arthur clapped him on the back. "Lachlan will be well pleased by the match you've made. Strengthening the bonds between the MacLeans and MacLeods holds great importance to him."

"I didnae marry her for that reason."

"Aye, I'm well aware." His grin widened.

"I only hope Rory will come to see so as well." It should be his task to inform Rory of their vows, except he couldn't take the risk of speaking to him this day when he needed to be away within mere hours.

He sat at the side table and picked up his spoon. The mouth-watering scent of seafood stew wafted around him. Annie adored seafood, particularly fresh fish.

From his wrist sheath, he removed his dagger, speared a sliver of beef from his trencher and bit into it. "I'll need to ensure Rory is warned about the MacDonalds. At the inn, I overheard a conversation between Hugh and one of his warriors. They were the ones following her."

"I suspected a MacDonald would have been behind her stalking." Arthur rolled his shirtsleeves up. "You might be interested to hear James has yet to return."

"He should have by now."

"Aye, I shall see if I can uncover his whereabouts. The fact he's still missing does no' sit well."

"Check if his warriors have returned."

"Will do."

Arthur left and Colin fetched additional weapons from his trunk and afterward, left in search of Rory. After hunting down his captain, he discovered Rory remained behind closed doors with the king. He paced the antechamber near the great hall as Rory's man closed the door. "I've learnt of a threat to Annie by the MacDonalds. I want one of your men watching over her at all times."

"Of course. I've no' long returned from assigning a guard to her for this eve's ball." Rory's captain palmed the hilt of his sword. "The MacDonalds are always scheming. We'll remain vigilant."

"Make sure you do." Still on edge, regardless her safety was assured, he left the man and returned to his chamber to dress. He donned the black robe, slipped the white mask in place and opened his door to find Arthur waiting in the same attire, his green gaze watchful behind his mask's eye cutouts. "Is there any sign of James?" he asked Arthur.

"I overheard one of his warriors speak of a chest illness. He remains at The King's Tavern to recover."

"The longer James stays away, the better." Colin slid his hood over his head. "Now I need to find my wife."

They joined an excited and raucous crowd of extravagantly costumed guests heading along the passageway. In the great hall, hundreds and hundreds of people swarmed the area, double or triple the usual number. Hell, finding Annie in this gathering wouldn't be easy. So many women wore wigs, and half those here now sported his wife's distinctive long white-blond hair.

"This is interesting." Arthur muffled as he gripped the lower edge of his mask. "Where is your lady? What does she wear?"

"I've no idea, and I should have asked. Let's separate, and if you find her first, signal me."

"Aye, I shall." Arthur walked off into the crowd.

Colin eased around the throng toward the trestle tables pressed against the wall. The tables overflowed with large platters of food, from sweet meats to pastries presented on fine silver and glass tiered stands. Sugared fruits preserved from the summer, many of Annie's favorites, had him searching for her first amongst the guests partaking of those delicacies. Annie would be driven to see all on offer, to taste and enjoy, but she wasn't anywhere in sight.

Moving along, he sidestepped past three blond-haired women wearing scandalously little. Their exposed bellies were adorned with gold chains and glittering precious gems. Low on their hips, their vibrant skirts of reds and pinks flared to the floor in sheer folds. The same wispy fabric covered their breasts and tied off at their backs with long ribbons and dangling beads which chimed as they swayed to the piper's music floating through from the adjoining room. They were dressed as belly dancers from the orient. He'd heard of the people who lived in the east on a land of shifting sands, the weather so scorching they wore very little clothing. The translucent fabric of their costume also covered their lower faces and hid their identities, although none of the women had Annie's beautiful midnight-blue eyes.

More guests swarmed into the hall and as he searched for her, he tugged the tight neckline of his robe. If only he could jump onto one of the burgundy padded chairs at the side of the hall and shout Annie's name, except calling attention to himself was the last thing he needed. Aye, he'd search for Rory or Elizabeth instead. Surely they would lead him to Annie.

* * * *

Annie eased back against the bright yellow plastered wall decorated with stunning tapestries of landscape and hunting scenes. A man attired in domino wearing a black hooded robe and full white mask circled the great hall clenching and unclenching his fists. Colin had said he'd be dressed as a monk, but each of the monks she'd stopped and spoken to thus far hadn't been him. Maybe he was still preparing all he needed to for this eve, except why did the man in the black robe intrigue her so? Turning her gaze from him, she searched the crowd again for any sign of Rory or Elizabeth. She hadn't a clue what either of them would be wearing, and so far, she'd not seen them as well.

Restless, she pushed off the wall, intent on halting the robed man and curbing her curiosity.

"Annie?" Another black-robed guest in domino stepped in front of her, his deep brogue giving his identity away.

"Arthur." She hugged him, and likely far too exuberantly before she stepped back and straightened her hand-painted mask. The full facial adornment was elaborately detailed and gave her the fine features of Cleopatra, Egypt's legendary queen with her catlike eyes and ruby red lips. Her wig of dark brown locks was coiled high on her head and encircled by a headdress of gold plumes, while the wispy skirts of her white chiffon gown brushed the floorboards. "Thank goodness you found me."

"What are you wearing?" Arthur's vivid green eyes widened behind his white eye cutouts.

"I'm Cleopatra." She fluttered her hand over the seductively plunging bodice with its matching deep V cut into the back, a gown that was impossible to wear with any undergarments. Her brisk movement sent the thin shoulder straps with their wing-like layer of chiffon swishing softly across her skin, as well as the gold bangles at her wrist jangling. Never had she felt so nervous and wickedly decadent at the same time. The thin fabric hugged her body with a silky touch and allowed the heat of the room to pass right over her. "I'm looking for my Caesar."

"As he's looking for you."

"Pardon me, my queen." A warrior wearing sandals with iron studs and armor made of metal strips over a red woolen tunic bowed before her. "May I have this dance?"

"Nay, you may no'," Arthur bit out as he whisked her onto the dance floor. "Where is your guard?"

"Near the balcony doors, dressed in the same fashion as you." At least two score of the men here were attired in domino. "Colin was supposed to be dressed as a monk but I've no' seen him."

"A change of plans. Blending in with the crowd seemed a better choice. He wears what I do." Frowning, he peered over her shoulder and she followed his gaze. "Is that the king?" he asked, astounded.

"Aye, whispers are running rampant he's dressed as Ares, the Greek god of war." King James VI was richly costumed in full body armor, a shield and sword in hand and a magnificent red-plumed iron nasal helm adorning his head. "He looks magnificent with that full mask of white and gold."

"Dinnae let Colin hear you say that." Arthur led her through the dance's intricate moves with practiced ease. "Did you hear about James?"

"Aye, he's taken ill. One of his warriors gave my maid his apologies. I was told he does no' wish to spread his sickness about, but that he'll return as soon as he's able to ride. What of you? Have you heard any gossip swirling about the time I spent alone with James at the tavern?"

"Everyone is too excited by the ball to worry about such a thing. You're very fortunate with the timing." He leaned forward. "Colin told me of your handfast. My congratulations."

"Thank you." She couldn't hold back her smile. "Is everything sorted for this eve? I'm aware of your plans."

"Aye, but for one last matter. I need a maid to deliver the tower guardsmen a celebratory tankard of ale at midnight."

"Whatever for?"

"Stirred into the brew will be a sleeping potion."

"If there's no danger to the servant, then I could ask my own maid. She'd no' speak a word of what she's done."

"Can she wear a mask? Most of the serving lasses have done so this eve and I had intended to ask one of them under the guise that the Captain of the Guard had made the request."

"Of course she can wear a mask. I have more than one in my trunk. Where do you need her to meet you?"

"Your chamber would be best, a quarter afore twelve and

no later. I'll procure the ale now and leave it hidden in your room. When she delivers the drinks, I'll be watching over her. I'll no' leave her alone."

"I know you—" Someone brushed against her from behind then slid his large hands over her hips. Colin. She would know his touch anywhere. "Oh, it appears our dance is done."

"Aye, your Caesar is here." Arthur bowed and moved away into the crowd.

"I've missed you." Warm words whispered in her ear. "Let's take a turn outside."

"I thought you'd never ask." She slid her hand through the crook of his arm and as she walked past her guard, stopped and whispered to him, "'Tis my guardian. You may wait here."

Her MacLeod guard nodded.

Colin steered her outside and into the dark recesses of the palace's moonlit garden. He pressed her against a wide trunk, tipped his mask up and stared into her eyes. "I never would have guessed you'd have worn a wig."

"I couldnae find you either, no' when I searched for a monk."

"A change of plans." Slowly, he traced a finger down the deep V of her bodice then leaned in and nuzzled her neck. "I cannae believe you are wearing something so risqué. You cannae unmask with this costume on and bring your good name into question."

"No one's good name is brought into question once the masks are removed." She slid her mask off, wrapped her arms around his neck and leaned into him. "Thank you for my gift. The rose was beautiful."

"I wish I could give you one each day." He nipped her skin then laved it with his tongue.

"Mmm, so do I." She more than wished it.

"Dance with me." He slipped his arms around her waist, tucked her cheek against his chest and swayed slowly to the gentle melody of the tune drifting on the breeze.

"This is no' how one dances."

"'Tis the way I wish to dance with you." He rubbed his body against hers.

"Oh, I like it." She stroked down his arms and tangled her fingers with his. "Are you ready for this eve?"

"As I'll ever be."

"How will I know all has gone well?"

"There's no way for me to send you word." He backed her deeper into the shadows where thick bushes rose either side of them. He eased one finger under her shoulder strap and slid the flimsy chiffon down her arm. Her nipple puckered in the cold and she ached for the warmth of his mouth on her. "You are barely dressed."

"And you are making it more so."

"I long to touch you." He cupped her breast, rubbed his thumb sensuously over the peak then dipped his head and drew the bud deep inside his mouth. He laved it with attention, until her knees wobbled and she clutched his broad shoulders. He was so big and strong, and all hers.

"Colin." She caught his face and brought his mouth to hers. She kissed him, one breathtaking kiss she hoped he wouldn't forget as he headed out on his mission. "Come back to me once all is done."

"I will." He slid her shoulder strap back into place. "I wish I never had to leave."

"I wish it too." A shooting star flew in a wide arc across the sky and she closed her eyes to claim a wish on it. "I wish we were no' about to be parted. And I wish for a honeymoon, where there are no chiefs to rescue and no' a soul to disturb us."

"You shall have your honeymoon, the moment I come for you." He kissed her closed eyelids. "'Tis time. I must be away."

"You'll be careful?" She opened her eyes, slid her mask back into place as he did the same with his.

"Always." He guided her down the trail and back inside to where Arthur waited next to her guardsman. Colin nodded at Arthur. "Take Annie back to her chamber." To the guardsman, he said, "Ensure you collect Mistress MacLeod from her chamber in the morn. She's no' to roam Holyrood's halls without a guard."

She squeezed Colin's fingers. "I promise to be careful."

"And 'tis my job to ensure you do so. Take care, scamp." He dipped his head and left. Weaving through the crowd, he disappeared, and well before she was ready to let him go.

"We too must leave." Arthur took her elbow and steered her from the hall. "Let's find your maid."

They passed a stream of servants carrying trays with goblets of wine to be raised at midnight to celebrate the unmasking. Picking up her pace, she hurried to her room, only her maid wasn't there as she should have been. "Mayhap she's in Elizabeth's chamber."

"I'll go and check." Arthur left and returned moments later shaking his head. "Where else could she be?"

"There's a possibility she got called away to aid the palace staff."

"Then I'll have to deliver the ale myself. I'm running out of time to find another maid who might deliver it for me." He picked up the tray holding the pitcher and tankards from her side table.

"Will they accept it from you?"

"I can all but try."

"Arthur, nay. Allow me to deliver it. I'll change into my simplest gown. I have a plain white mask I could exchange for this one." She wouldn't be the cause of Colin, Arthur, or his men getting caught. "I willnae be recognizable, and no one will guess the maid was me."

"That's—"

"Surely 'tis best for the guards to slumber rather than for

you and Colin to take the tower by force. Turn around." He did and she removed the gold-plumed headdress from her wig then slipped behind the screen and changed into a navy kirtle with a knotted belt. She tossed a black and gray plaid over her shoulders and in the looking glass, placed the new mask over her face. "All right. What do you think?"

Arthur turned and studied her. He slowly nodded. "You do look like one of the maids, although Colin will kill me if he discovers I involved you and no' a servant."

"I'll be in and out in no time, and he none the wiser." She raced past him before he could change his mind. "Come."

He mumbled as he joined her, clearly not liking what he'd had to agree to.

Around the perimeter of the bailey, they crept until they reached the circular tower. Four guardsmen walked out the door, and she and Arthur slunk into a darkened corner along the midnight-shrouded stone wall.

"That'll be the change of the guards," Arthur whispered in her ear. "Tell the new guardsman you've brought a celebratory drink. That the Captain of the Guard requested it from the kitchens. Set the tray down and leave, immediately. I dinnae want you in there any longer than the time it takes for you to do that. Are we clear?"

"Very, but what if they dinnae partake of the ale?"

"That's no concern of yours. In and out. Make it quick." He glanced across the bailey toward the stables where something within the shadows caught his eye. Three men crept toward them. "Damn. 'Tis Colin with Ian and Murdock. Go now, lass, afore the captain arrives."

She draped her shawl over her head, took the tray from his hands and walked into the tower. The first pull of air into her lungs had her gasping for breath. The air was so rotten, her stomach heaved. Ignoring the stench as best she could, she stepped up to the barred door. Goodness, how on earth did Colin expect to get through here if not by ensuring the guards' compliance first?

"Excuse me," she called out. "I bring refreshments."

A warrior in a padded leather war coat scraped the steel door open and leered at her through stringy black hair. Behind him, a single candle-lit lantern hooked on the wall cast an eerie glow over the blackened gray-stone. "What do ye want, lass?"

"The Captain of the Guard sent me with ale. He thought you too might like to celebrate the king's masquerade."

"Over there will be fine." He jerked his head toward the table near the stairwell.

"And the other guardsmen?" No matter what Arthur had instructed, she couldn't leave without ensuring the guards had all been served. Colin's life could well depend on it.

"Above-stairs." He closed the barred door and turned the lock with a loud clunk, enclosing her inside with him. "I'm right thirsty. Pour me a tankard."

"Could you call the others? The captain insisted you all partake." She set the tray down with a rattle, poured him a mug and handed it across.

"Aye, I can call them." He ambled to the stairs, took a hearty gulp of his drink and bellowed, "Lads, we have us some ale and a fine lass to serve it, compliments of the captain."

She stepped around the wonky-legged table, putting it squarely between her and the coming guards as she poured another three drinks. Across the station, something moved beyond the slots in the barred entrance door. Golden eyes glinted from under a dark hood. Colin. Drat. Arthur must have told her she was the maid.

"What is ye name, lass?" The guard leaned one shoulder against the grimy wall nearest her.

"Lizzie," she uttered, choosing the most common name amongst the staff. "Is there just the four of you then?"

"Aye, is that nay enough for you?" Suggestive words, ones

that made her shiver with revulsion. Oh goodness, what had she gotten herself into?

Footsteps pounded down the stairs and two chainmail-clad warriors strode in. The walls of the guards' station encroached in on her as it filled with large men. Swiftly, she handed each of the warriors a drink and waited as they bumped their tankards together and drank.

"Thank the captain for us, lass," one of the warrior's grunted as he wiped his top lip, his gaze on her.

"I will."

"We'll take these drinks upstairs. We've our duties to attend to." The two disappeared the way they'd come.

Alone again with the first warrior, she said, "There's still one guardsman I've no' served."

"He'll be busy, otherwise he would've come." The guard plopped down on an overturned crate and yawned. He kicked out his legs and the keys looped around his belt clinked.

She itched to grab them, to toss them through the bars to Colin so he'd have no issue getting inside. Instead, she held her place. "Could you open the door then? The kitchens are busy with the ball in full swing and I'll be needed in the great hall."

"Aye, in a moment." Groggily, he lifted his head.

"Please, open the door. I dinnae wish to get in trouble." She stepped up to the door.

"I—I—" He staggered to his feet and swayed. "I'm com—" He tripped and toppled into her, squishing her between him and the hard wall. He mumbled as he tried to push himself upright. "I cannae keep my…" His eyes slid shut and he fell in a crashing heap to the floor.

"Annie," Colin rasped. "Get. Here. Now."

"I'll find the key." She shoved against the hefty warrior's side and rolled him from his front onto his back to free the chained keys from underneath him. The man was like a rock.

"Hurry." Colin fisted the bars. "I'm going to kill Arthur for allowing you in here."

"Nay, he told me to get in and out quickly. This isnae his fault when 'twas I who stayed."

"I still intend to kill him."

"Duly noted," Arthur groaned as he stepped in beside Colin and glared at her. "You dinnae listen to instructions. Get those keys and do it fast. If aught had happened to you, I'd never have forgiven myself."

"Where are your other men?" she asked Colin as she unhooked the keys from the warrior's belt.

"Keeping watch outside. Ian will take you back to your chamber, and once there, you will lock yourself inside until the morn when your MacLeod guardsman is due to arrive. Do. You. Understand. Me?"

"Perfectly." She removed her mask as she hurried to the door so she could see better. "There's one guard who never took any of the ale." She tried the first key in the lock, but it didn't turn.

"Give them here." Colin snuck them from her hand and through the bars worked each key in turn until the lock popped open. The door swung wide then he clamped her against his chest, so tight she lost her breath with a whoosh. To Arthur, he bit out, "Upstairs with you, and dinnae let any of the guards kill you. That's my job."

"Aye, Captain." Arthur dashed past them in a whirl of black, his sword in hand as he vanished up the stairwell.

Colin tipped up her chin and looked into her eyes. "Go straight to Ian, and keep to the shadows. I'll see you at Dunvegan."

"I'll be waiting."

He released her and bolted upstairs, gone before she could whisper another word.

Chapter 6

Without a lantern to light his way, Colin negotiated the cramped stairwell in the dark of night, his sword at the ready. Somewhere up ahead, a snore broke the quiet, and as he stepped onto the landing, he found one of the guards who'd drunken the ale lying slumped across the floor. Two down, two to go. He tapped Arthur's arm with his sword. "How much potion did you give them?"

"I poured the entire vial into the pitcher instead of only a few drops. I didnae want to take the chance they only napped. We need some light in here." Arthur wedged his dirk under one of the thin boards across the narrow window and popped it free. A trace of moonlight shone in and beamed over a third warrior lying prone halfway up the next flight of stairs.

Colin sheathed his sword, grabbed the man's feet and hauled him down. Kneeling, he checked his breathing. "'Tis slow but steady."

"Then we've only one more to find, the warrior Annie didnae serve." Arthur crept upstairs.

Following him with his senses on full alert, Colin reached the top landing and surveyed the passageway ahead. The darkened corridor remained bare, although Lachlan's cell door remained propped wide open. "He waits for us in there."

"Damn. He must have discovered his fellow guards had gone down afore we did." Arthur tugged his hood lower over his mask.

"I'll go first." Sword raised, Colin snuck into the cell lit only by a single candle.

"Come one step closer, and I'll slit his throat." The guard held Lachlan in a choke hold, his blade pressed to his neck and his chief the man's living shield.

"Hand MacLean over. He does no' deserve to be here, kept in the dark like some rat and fed the scraps King James decides he might have." Colin nodded at Arthur. "Check on the MacDonalds. Make sure their door remains locked."

"They're no' there," the guard snickered, his long hair covering one beady black eye. "Both were taken to more comfortable quarters in the palace. Apparently they're more receptive to the king's terms than the Chief of MacLean has been."

"You lie. Donald and Angus MacDonald would never relent."

"He speaks the truth," Lachlan rasped against the blade at his throat. "Just afore dusk they were taken away. I was told they'd agreed to pay the hefty fines and have sworn their obedience to the king. They've also stated they'll no' oppose the government and when summoned to Edinburgh, return within twenty days. Is that you, Malcolm?" Lachlan shot Arthur a warning look as he returned. "And is that you, Munroe?"

"Aye, 'tis me Munroe," Arthur answered him. "We've come to free you."

"Then you should know"—Lachlan slid his gaze back to Colin—"the king has offered to look into the return of my land on the Isle of Islay. Should he do so, and if all works in my favor, then I intend to accede to his demands to get the Rhinns back."

Colin could barely believe it. For too many years to count, Lachlan had been fighting the MacDonald of Dunnyveg for the return of that land. Lachlan had lost the Rhinns to Angus MacDonald when his father had gambled it away during the short five years he'd been chief, but Lachlan had always insisted his father had lost it illegally. Hell, 'twas no wonder Lachlan had changed his mind. The MacLeans might once again own a portion of Islay. 'Twould be worth the hefty fines and summoning to Edinburgh for such a triumph. "Then I take it you would like us to leave, Chief?"

"Aye, a rescue is no longer needed."

Lachlan MacLean was one of the greatest strategists, and if he now wished to negotiate with the king for his land on Islay's west coast, then Colin wouldn't stop him. He dipped his head and stepped back. "Then I bid you a good night."

"Aye, but, Malcolm, it would pay for you and Munroe to get away from here as fast as you can."

"That we will. Virtue mine honor." He pulled the cell door shut. "Find me something solid enough to bar the door," he snapped at Arthur. He couldn't have the guard raising the alert, and locking him in with Lachlan right now was his only alternative.

"Here." Arthur grabbed a plank of wood propped against the wall and slotted it through the shaft designed to bar the door should the lock be unusable.

"That should give us a few hours, I hope." Colin rushed down the corridor then traversed the tight stairwell as fast as he could. Outside, Ian and Murdock waited in the shadows. "Where's Annie?" he asked Ian.

"In her chamber, safe and well," Ian tipped his cloaked hood back enough for his eyes to show. "Where's the chief?"

"He's been offered a deal by the king he does no' intend to turn down. The Rhinns in exchange for acceding to his demands. Which means you need to leave, quickly. Return to the faerie stones and wait for us there."

"You're no' leaving with us?" Ian grasped his arm. "'Twill be an easy guess for the guards to look first at you and Arthur as the culprits for this attempt on the tower."

"The chief is still here and we've remained masked the entire time. He also gave the guard false names, so provided Arthur and I can merge back in amongst the guests, who's to say we've no' been in the great hall the entire time?" And if he had the chance to remain behind, for Annie's sake, he'd damn well do it. His wife knew how to find trouble too well on her own.

"The risk is too great."

"Have you been sighted?" he asked Ian.

"No one can identify us."

"Then feel free to expose your MacLean plaids as you ride out. Two of Lachlan's warriors must be sighted leaving here." Colin clasped Ian's forearms in a firm warrior's hold before doing the same with Murdock. "We may need a few days. Take care."

The two warriors slunk away into the dark.

Colin grasped Arthur's shoulder. "Are you with me?"

"Aye, and 'tis best when we leave, we do so with your wife. Mayhap you should even change into your monk's habit. 'Twould be best if neither of us remained attired in domino as the guard saw us."

"A sound idea. Let's go." Against the castle wall, Colin slid through the shadows then hastened along the maze of passageways. In his chamber, he stripped off his robe and mask as Arthur did the same, then donned his brown monk's habit and tied the leather strings around his waist. "Are you ready to face the masses?"

Arthur tucked his tunic into his dark leather trews. "This will need to do for me. Let's hope we dinnae get caught."

* * * *

Annie couldn't sit still after Ian had raced her back to her chamber and instructed her to bolt the door and get rid of the clothing she'd worn. No link must be made between her and the maid who'd delivered the ale. As quick as she could, she lit the fire, stripped off her kirtle and tossed her clothes and the wig into the flames.

As it burned to ashes, she shakily dressed in a midnight-blue gown edged in black satin. Wishing for an escape, she paced her chamber. She needed to know if Colin had gotten past all the guards and reached his chief without issue. Even now, did he ride across the country for Duart Castle? Her stomach tossed and turned and her thoughts wouldn't settle. Aye, she should follow Colin's instructions and remain where she was, but the castle was filled with guests roaming about and it would take mere minutes to check the stables for his mount.

She grabbed her black fur cloak and swung it over her shoulders. She'd take the utmost care, discover if his horse remained, then return.

With her softly lined fur hood covering her head, she snuck out the door.

"Well, well, if it isnae Annie MacLeod." A warrior with a red bulbous nose wearing the MacDonald plaid under a steel-studded war coat eased out of the darkened alcove next to her door. "You've been busy this eve, dressed as Cleopatra one moment, then a lowly maid the next. Now you appear as if you're ready to wander about again, yet this time unescorted."

"Who are you?"

"Hugh MacDonald at your service."

"I've heard of you." A man she had no desire to stand about chatting to. "Excuse me." She hurried down the passageway.

"James is courting you, but he's no' for you."

"He's no' courting me, and I agree."

"Good." He offered her his arm as he kept pace but she ignored the gesture. "Allow me to escort you to wherever it is you're going."

"No thank you. I'll escort myself." A buzz of voices echoed toward her from the great hall. She wasn't in the middle of the woods, but a crowded palace swarming with guests and guardsmen. Aye, she'd find one of her MacLeod warriors and be done with Hugh MacDonald.

"Take my arm, my lady, and if I were you, I wouldnae draw any attention to us should the opportunity arise."

"Are you threatening me?" She hastened her step as she searched for one of her kin.

"You should have taken more care this eve." He snorted. "Particularly after your jaunt to the tower, and if I were to hazard a guess at to the identities of the other men I saw you with, I'd have to say they were Colin and Arthur MacLean."

"I—I—" A chill shuddered through her. Hugh MacDonald knew too much.

"Allow me to allay your fears. The men you seek have returned to the ball."

Colin would never have done so, not after he'd rescued his chief.

"They also left the tower empty handed."

"What?"

"Take care. Dinnae draw any attention to us. If you do, Colin and Arthur MacLean will be hanging from the king's noose at daybreak, and if that happens, 'twill be because you've forced my hand and I've had no choice but to expose them." He gripped her elbow, tugged her through the doors and across the inner courtyard.

"What are you doing?"

"Ensuring you save your kin. I take it you wish to confirm their steads are here?" MacDonald steered her inside the stables, led her past two lads brushing down the guests' horses, and toward the rear.

Colin and Arthur's horses remained in their stalls. Hugh had told her the truth. Colin hadn't left.

"Wait here." Hugh stepped across the dusty corridor, stirring up loose hay scattered across the hard-packed ground. He clapped a warrior on the back, and said, "Fergus, gather four of our men, those loyal only to me and no' James."

"Aye, Captain." Fergus jogged past her.

Their voices sent shivers down her spine. She brushed up against Colin's destrier and scratched between his stallion's silky black ears. "Where are they, and what happened to them?" she whispered to the animal, hoping an answer would present itself, somehow and some way.

The war horse let out a throaty snort and knocked its muzzle into her shoulder as if pushing her to send her on her way.

"We'll be leaving soon." Hugh saddled his horse.

"Then go. I'll no' stop you."

"I would prefer it if you traveled with me." He mounted, took his horse's reins and nodded at Fergus as he arrived with his men. "Aid the lady, Fergus. She wishes to ride with us."

"Nay, I—" She squealed as the warrior caught her around the waist and boosted her into the saddle in front of Hugh. "You cannae do this."

"Oh, I believe I can," he rasped in her ear. "And if you dinnae oblige and come willingly, then I'll discuss what I've learnt this eve with the king. Do you wish to keep Colin MacLean from the dungeons, or do you prefer to send him to an early death?" He nudged his horse out into the bailey.

Speak up and save herself, or remain quiet and save Colin.

There wasn't even an option.

"I'm the Chief of MacLeod's cousin," she snapped at him. "You cannae abduct me without severe repercussions."

"This is no' an abduction, but a willing agreement to a courtship."

"I've agreed to naught."

"Aye, you have." Arms tight around her, he urged his horse

out the gates, right under the watchful eye of the guards patrolling the barbican, and she could do nothing about it.

"Where are you taking me?"

"To Dunscaith on Skye where I can keep you secured within the MacDonald stronghold. James is too lenient toward the enemy and longs for peace at the expense of our own clan, whereas I shall fight against clan MacLean as my chief does. For that, we require an alliance with Rory MacLeod, and you are the perfect solution."

"Your chief cannae fight while he's in the tower."

"Donald and Angus were removed from the tower earlier this eve and taken to secure quarters in the palace. They've both agreed to the king's demands and will soon be released. And when my chief returns to his clan, he will hear of our alliance by marriage and be well-pleased." He thumped his heels into his stead's flanks, urging his horse to a faster pace. He raced through the city, his men close behind.

"That's a marriage I will never agree to, no' when I've already handfasted with another."

"Handfast vows are easily broken." He shook his head and snorted in disgust. "Did you speak them with MacLean?"

"Aye."

"Then those vows are irrelevant. The clergyman at Dunscaith will gladly hear you speak true marriage vows with me. You will embrace your new role as my wife. Make no mistake about it."

* * * *

Colin snuck into the great hall with Arthur. So many people enthusiastically greeted each other as they finally learnt who was who. Several wives giggled and fanned their flushed faces as their husbands found them.

"What's your plan of attack now?" Arthur asked him.

"We need to find Rory and ensure we're seen." Across the hall, a dark blond-haired warrior in full Viking costume with his claymore holstered across his back and his battle-axe belted at his side drew his attention.

"'Tis a good plan. Let's hope it works." Arthur rubbed his neck. "I'm no' keen to have the king's noose around my neck."

"Neither am I, and I do believe that's Rory." He weaved around the chattering groups and blew out a long breath as Rory turned, his mask swinging from one hand and his face clear to see. Colin grasped Rory's shoulder. "About time I found you."

Rory's gaze swept over him. "Ha. You are the last man I'd expected to see dressed as a monk. You love to war, no' make peace."

"Colin, you are a surprising sight." Elizabeth smiled, the feathery fairy wings at the back of her white gown fluttering in the breeze from the open balcony doors. "Have you seen Annie now all have unmasked? There are so many here, and the costumes so wonderful, but I dinnae even know what my own niece wears."

"She's outfitted as Cleopatra, but she grew tired and retired to her chamber."

"Then I shall go and check on her." Elizabeth leaned in, her voice low as she continued, "I've no' heard any rumors circulating about her and James. Have you?"

"James is still at the tavern. He took ill."

She gasped. "Oh, how terrible, but what a stroke of good luck for us."

Rory crossed his wide arms. "Aye, and glad I am too to see James has no' been able to cause a stir."

"I had Annie back afore dawn." Colin tipped his head toward Arthur. "Go with Elizabeth and ensure Annie is well. Tell her I'll be there soon to talk to her."

"Will do." Arthur offered Elizabeth his arm and led her away.

Colin rubbed his chest. His heart still wasn't beating right, not since the moment he'd discovered Annie had been the maid delivering the spiked ale. They would have words, and Annie was about to learn he'd never allow her to attempt such a thing again.

"You look worried, Colin." Rory's brow drew down. "My captain passed on your message that the MacDonalds are scheming, although that isnae unusual. We've always maintained vigilance around them."

"Aye, but there's far more we need to speak of than just the MacDonalds." Now he had the chance to inform Rory of his handfast vows with Annie, he needed to do so. Aye, it would be best if the news came from him, and afore too much time had passed. Motioning toward the doors, he said, "If you dinnae mind, we need privacy."

"Of course." Rory strode from the hall.

Colin followed him down the shadowy passageway and into a private antechamber. He sat in the lavishly upholstered burgundy chair next to the window.

Rory took the seat opposite him and planted his elbows on his knees, his hands pressed together and his battle-axe glowing blood-red at his side from the fire's flickering flames.

Patting his ever-present side sword, Colin hoped like hell he wouldn't need to raise it. "Annie has found herself a husband, a man I heartily approve of."

"Then it cannae be a MacDonald." Rory tapped one foot. "You look uneasy. If you heartily approve then who is it? And why has she no' said a word to me?"

"Because I'm the man she wishes to wed."

Rory's fingers twitched and his nostrils flared. "That's impossible. You're her cousin, her guardian. She cannae wed you."

"Third cousin, and there is no law against such a union."

"Nay, her father entrusted you with her safety and welfare, as he did me. Guardians dinnae marry their wards, you included." Rory stood, his chest pumped out.

Colin rose and stood eye-to-eye with the warrior he'd always called a friend. "We've already spoken vows. She's my handfast wife, and I willnae give her up."

"Damn it, Colin. You've abused my trust. You and Annie grew up together and you're as close as siblings."

"The feelings I have for her are far removed from that of a brother toward his sister."

"Then they are feelings you need to ignore, and if you've taken advantage of her and consummated the handfast, I'll kill you, right here and right now."

"Rory," Elizabeth cried his name from the doorway, her hand fluttering wildly over her chest. "How could you say such a thing?"

Arthur urged her inside and shut the paneled door behind them. "I have news."

"Then it'll have to wait." Rory slammed Colin into the plastered wall behind him. The wall rattled and shook at the brutal impact. Squeezing his throat, Rory rasped in his ear, "Did. You. Bed. Her?"

Colin thrust his knee into Rory's groin and took him down to the floor. "That's none of your damn business."

"Oh goodness." Elizabeth plopped into the chair. "Rory, Annie loves Colin. They make a perfect match."

"Arthur, get Annie in here now." Rory rolled Colin off him and came up on top. "I want to hear all of this from her own mouth."

"She wasnae in her chamber. Her cape was gone and there was no sign of her."

"Hell." Colin bucked Rory off and jumped to his feet. "Arthur, rouse Rory's men to aid you and check the great hall, the private rooms, anywhere and everywhere. She has to be here somewhere."

"Aye, Captain." Arthur raced out the door.

Colin was right behind him.

Rory caught him up as he sprinted toward the stables. "She cannae have gone far. My warriors would know." Rory grabbed one of the stable hands as they flew inside. "Have you seen Mistress MacLeod?"

"Aye, my laird. She rode out the gate a few minutes ago with Hugh MacDonald and his warriors. She went willingly enough. They ride for Skye."

"She would never have gone willingly." Colin whistled to Arthur as his man ran across the bailey with a half dozen of Rory's warriors. "Hugh MacDonald has her. We're riding out now," he bellowed to Arthur.

Colin mounted his steed and galloped out the gates. Every moment counted. There could be no delay.

Rory pounded in beside him, his gaze fierce as they raced through the city streets and along the route toward Skye. "At any time Annie could've called out and the palace guards would have prevented MacDonald from leaving with her. This makes no sense."

"MacDonald has to be holding something against her. She'd never leave otherwise."

"And what could that possibly be?" Rory demanded.

Annie was an innocent, although one embroiled in his endeavor to free his chief. Aye, and the timing of her kidnapping was too coincidental for it not to have something to do with him. "My chief is locked away and needs to be freed, something which would have happened this eve."

"What are you saying?"

"I discovered, and far too late, that Lachlan intends to capitulate to the king's demands for the return of his land on Islay."

"And Annie knew about your plans?"

"There is little she does no' find a way to learn."

"Then this is your fault. You led her straight to danger's door. You gave MacDonald some form of control over her.

Naught else makes sense." Rory's hair whipped about his shoulders.

Colin could say nothing to defend himself. He'd allowed this to happen, and if Annie was harmed in any way for his terrible mistake, he'd never forgive himself.

Their party of warriors left the city behind and rode hard across the moors.

"Fresh tracks," Arthur shouted.

Aye, several hoof prints were embedded deep into the soil, easy to spot now the dawn's rising sun had lightened the skies. Ahead, the forest lay with a silver tinge along the treetops, and somewhere within, Annie rode, captured by his enemy.

"I'm coming," he whispered to her, his heart a pounding mess. "I'm coming."

* * * *

The rising sun sent the night's frosty air to ground, although the welcoming warmth did little to ease the deep chill in Annie's bones. At her back, Hugh MacDonald was a solid presence as he galloped down the forest trail scattered with autumn leaves, his men pounding behind them. She wriggled and tried to stretch as her muscles protested the hours of confinement. She'd repeatedly requested a stop, but he'd not once accommodated her. Now she ached, everywhere, her heart included.

"Fergus," Hugh called to his man. "Ride ahead to the burn and check all is well. If it is, we'll stop and water our horses there."

"Aye, Captain." Fergus rode past then disappeared around a bend in the trail.

"You're rather quiet," Hugh rumbled in her ear.

She wriggled forward, instilling whatever space she could between them. "I've naught to say to a man who thinks 'tis acceptable to abduct an innocent lady."

"An innocent lady who'll soon be my wife. Watch your tongue, Annie. I willnae abide being spoken to like a common thief. A quiet and accepting demeanor in a wife would be appreciated."

"Then you abducted the wrong lass. My tongue is rather forthright." She wanted to hit him.

Fergus rode back and Hugh slowed his mount after the warrior motioned all was well.

"It appears you'll be granted a short respite." Hugh pulled his horse to a stop next to Fergus's near a gurgling stream. He jumped down, looped his destrier's reins over a low branch and held out his hands to her. "Allow me to aid you."

"Your kind of aid, I dinnae require." She dismounted on the other side, and even though her legs shook, she rubbed her lower limbs and brought the sensation back.

"Are you all right?" Arms crossed, Hugh loomed over her.

"Some water to quench my thirst and a walk to loosen my legs would be appreciated." Her freedom even more so, not that MacDonald would be granting her that. Watchful of her step, she negotiated the rocky bank then on her knees at the edge, scooped the chilly water and drank. The cold liquid hit her empty belly and she shuddered.

"It would pay for you to drink slowly."

"Leave me alone. You dinnae need to hover."

"There are dangers in the forest."

"And I'm well aware of them." Colin had drummed all the possible pitfalls into her since she'd been old enough to walk. She knew how to take care of herself.

"Lass, you must keep an open mind about our forthcoming marriage." The idiot perched on the moss covered rock next to her, kicked his booted feet out and arched a brow. "I dinnae care for your behavior."

"Too bad."

"We should speak, and afore we make Dunscaith." He scrubbed his bearded jaw. "I have a wee daughter. She's eight and lost her mother a year past. Her name is Beitris and she needs a firm hand. I'm afraid I've allowed her to get away with too much of late." He stared back down the trail. "I'm a hard man, lass, but I dinnae wish to be hard on you. For this alliance to work, I need you to accept what will be."

"I'm already wed."

"No' for long. You will repudiate your handfast vows afore we reach Dunscaith."

"I'll do no such thing, and you cannae intimidate me. I'm a MacLeod in case you missed that."

"I'm well aware, and one I intend to bed very soon."

"No' with my permission." She pushed to her feet. "Excuse me. I presume you willnae wish to stay for long and I must have some privacy to tend to my needs."

"You have five minutes, and remember, I will be watching."

"If you are, I'll clobber you." She hoped the threat worked, but regardless, she trod through the thick grass until she found a suitably dense bush to crouch behind. She sniffed and squeezed her eyes shut. Nay, she wouldn't cry. She had to remain strong. "I'm so sorry, Colin," she whispered as a tear escaped.

Leaves and bracken crackled behind her. She stiffened and held perfectly still.

Surely MacDonald wouldn't actually follow through on his threat to keep this close of an eye on her.

She cocked an ear as a pretty bird's trill reached her on the breeze, its precious chirps making her catch her breath. She'd know that call anywhere, had heard it countless times on Mull.

From behind a tree, Colin slithered out and along the grassy trail, his expression holding fierce determination. He eased in beside her, pressed one finger to her lips then rasped, "In the future, when I say to remain in your chamber, you will do so."

"Are you really here?" She clutched his face. Aye, he was real. "How did you find me?"

"We discovered you were missing mere minutes after you

left."

"We? Is Rory here?"

"He and his men are moving into position to take care of the other MacDonald warriors. Why'd you leave with him?"

"He knew you'd been at the tower, was aware of your attempt to free your chief. He said he'd tell the king of your involvement if I didnae go willingly."

"I'm sorry, Annie. I never intended for you to get caught in the middle of this war. Never again." He tipped his head toward the path he'd snuck along. "Arthur awaits farther back. I need you to stay as low as possible and crawl straight to him."

"You're going to battle Hugh alone?" She clung to him. "Please, even though he abducted me, I dinnae wish for the feud between the clans to escalate because of me."

"Are ye finished yet, my lady?" Hugh grated. He was close, too close.

"Go." Colin turned her by the shoulders, tipped her onto her belly and slid his sword free. "Now."

"He has a daughter and the child has no mother. If you kill him, she'll be without parents."

"The lass is of no concern to you, Annie." He pressed a soft kiss on her lips and nudged her to go.

"I grew up without my parents and I dinnae wish for his daughter to do so as well. Please, be careful." She had no choice but to leave. "And I mean no' one scratch, or I'll be very angry. You dinnae want to see me angry, Colin MacLean."

"Aye, scamp. I'll take care."

She scuttled through the underbrush, hating that she had to leave him.

"Come here, lass." Arthur stepped out from behind a trunk and scooped her into his arms.

"Put me down. I can find my own way to safety. Stay with Colin."

"Nay, I have to get you away from here afore I can rejoin

the captain. Hold tight." He lifted her higher against his chest and she seized his shoulders as he ran through the trees. Everything blurred and her head spun.

Colin's fierce battle cry rang out, and the chilling sound reverberated throughout the forest as her MacLeod kin joined in with his roar. So many men fighting, and all because of her.

As steel rang loud against steel, the grating clang had her shoving against Arthur's chest. "Put me down here. This is far enough. You have to go back, now."

"Aye, this should do." He glanced up into the dense foliage of a tree then boosted her into the safety of the wide bow, her position hidden.

"Go, please. I cannae lose Colin as I lost my parents. I'd never survive it."

"I'm going. Stay here." He dashed away.

Chapter 7

Colin thrust his sword high and blocked Hugh MacDonald's swift blow. The urge to kill the warrior for stealing Annie from him throbbed with deadly menace deep inside him. The MacDonalds were a thorn in his side, a constant threat against him and his kin.

"Where is she, MacLean?" Hugh's gaze glinted with animosity.

"Safely away, so I might end your life and then join her." He slammed his blade into Hugh's side.

Grunting, Hugh fell back a step. He grasped his side and eyed the long slice in his steel-studded war coat, a cut that hadn't quite drawn blood. "She's agreed to be my wife."

"Like hell she has."

"She's your cousin and ward."

"Third cousin, and as my ward, I've well and truly ensured her future."

"Fergus," Hugh shouted.

"Here." Fergus jumped the low brush and came in beside Hugh. "Rory MacLeod is here with as many warriors as us. The men fight."

"MacLean must die. He stands in my way." Hugh twirled

his blade and softened his footing. Fergus did the same, the two of them coming around either side of Colin.

"You're a blood-thirsty lot." Colin rocked on his heels as battle lust roared through him. "I'll enjoy ridding Scotland of the two of you."

"Strong words, MacLean. But futile," Hugh snorted.

Both MacDonalds advanced.

Hugh struck first and Colin spun and blocked the fierce blow. As Fergus attacked, Colin dropped low, kicked the warrior's shin and sent Fergus sprawling into a thorny bush.

Fergus shoved to his feet. "A dirty move, MacLean."

"And what do you call two warriors battling against one?" Colin fought, his claymore clashing against Hugh's blade and then Fergus's. Their blows were well-timed as they worked together against him.

"I'm here," Arthur yelled as he bounded into the fight.

"Is Annie safe?"

"Aye, Captain." Arthur shoved his back against Colin's then fought Fergus as he swung his sword. "I tossed her into a tree."

"She can scramble up and down trees in her sleep."

"Colin!" Annie shouted his name as she ran toward him, her white-blond hair streaming behind her. "No' a scratch. Do you hear me?"

"Get back." Damn it. He had to end this battle before she got any closer. He glared at Arthur. "Next time, tie her down."

"There willnae be a next time," Hugh smirked as he struck Colin's ribs.

Pain ricocheted and rattled his teeth from the brutal blow. Hell. He should've been paying attention to the fight and not his wife.

Annie screamed as Hugh swung again.

Colin barely caught the next blow. It knocked him onto his knees, their two blades crashing together a mere breath from his nose.

"You'll never wed my wife." Arms shaking, Colin shoved his two-handed sword hard against Hugh's and heaved to his feet. He sprang forward and fought. Annie needed him alive, and there was no greater incentive than to fight for her and their future together. He slammed his blade into Hugh's arm and blood spurted.

Hugh gripped his wound and yelled at Fergus for aid, except his man was of no use since Arthur had him on the ground, his knee planted into Fergus's back as he bound his arms with his leather belt and restrained him.

Colin slid his claymore tight against Hugh's throat. "You've lost the fight."

"Colin, nay." Annie clenched her midnight-blue skirts. "Please, I had to watch my parents die, and Hugh too has a child. Let the king decide their punishment."

"I prefer to hand out my own punishment." He pressed until blood oozed. "And I believe I shall make it as painful as possible."

All around the forest stilled as the sounds of the battle ceased. Rory emerged from the thick trees with heaving breaths, his claymore in one hand and battle-axe in the other. Blood dripped from both, as it did from the swords of his warriors who strode in beside him. "There are only these two left," Rory stated. "The others wouldnae concede to defeat."

Annie ran to Rory. "I cannae take anymore death. This has to stop."

"Lass, you should never have been brought into this feud." He pulled her into his arms. "Your husband has every right now to seek justice for your abduction."

"He told you about our vows?"

"Aye, but you must speak for yourself. Do you truly love him?"

"I do, with all my heart." She glanced at Colin. "Please,

spare these two men."

"They intended to kill us, Annie."

"You're better than them. You could end Hugh's life, or you could deliver him to the king."

Aye, but which should it be? Certainly death at his hand was almost too easy for Hugh. He should be made to suffer, and what with his abduction of Annie, any word Hugh now spoke against Colin would be considered naught but vindictive ramblings. He should be safe against anything Hugh said, but could he take that risk?

"'Tis up to you." Rory nodded at him as he wiped his axe on the grass and holstered it. "Although, you and your chief will have more sway with the king should you allow him to see justice is done. We're on the king's land, Colin. He wishes for the clans to make peace, for Scotland to be united as one."

More sway wouldn't hurt, particularly if it aided his chief in his negotiations, and Annie's pleading gaze, so filled with trust, tore at his heart. For him to take MacDonald's life in front of her, would dim that light. He lowered his blade. "For my wife's sake, we'll take these two in."

He shoved Hugh facedown into the dirt and one of Rory's warriors bounded across and restrained him with rope.

Rory called to his men. "'Tis been a long night and we've a long day ahead of us, but we willnae leave until we've buried the dead."

Annie sprang into Colin's arms and he caught her, barely planting one foot back in time to stop them both from tumbling to the ground. "You made the right choice."

"Aye, because now I have you, scamp, all of you."

"You've always had all of me." She smoothed one finger over his chin and frowned. "There's a bruise. When did you get this?"

"Rory didnae take the initial news of our handfast vows well."

"I should have been there when you told him."

"You can kiss it better if you like."

"I'd like very much." A mischievous glint lit her beautiful blue eyes as she lifted onto her toes and brushed her lips against his.

"The bruise is lower." He cupped her cheek as longing rushed through him.

"I was getting there." She kissed a scratch on his neck then nibbled along to his ear. "This could take a while afore I get to that bruise."

"Then we need more privacy." He scooped her into his arms and carried her deeper into the forest where they could be guaranteed just that. He sat on the lush grass surrounded by brush and rested back against a thick trunk with Annie in his lap. The sun's rays snuck through the thick foliage overhead and played across the ground. Unable to hold back, he kissed her. Damn. She tasted so sweet, and he'd missed her, in the worst possible way. He plundered her mouth as the need to be closer still drove him. Touching her, having her body pressed against his was heaven, a sensation he never wanted to be without. He stroked down her thigh then slid his hand under the blue velvet folds of her gown and caressed her soft flesh.

She writhed against him. "Should we be doing this out here?"

"We're alone, and I need to touch you, to know you're back in my arms." He trailed along her inner thigh and sighed as her heat pulsed, so close. Beyond aroused, he slid a finger inside her and rubbed her tight nub. "I'll remain alert."

"Colin." She pressed her hips higher. "I ache."

"And I shall ease that ache." Spreading her legs farther apart, he stroked deeper until she panted for breath.

"Kiss me, please," she whispered, arching into his touch.

He captured her mouth and allowed his desire for her to soar free. Her heartbeat thumped against his and below, he added another finger and thrust deeper until her channel tightened exquisitely around him. With his fingers alone, he drove her over the edge until she trembled in his arms.

She was all he'd ever longed for, the only woman he'd ever love.

Contentment and peace rolled through him. "My love, a lifetime with you will never be long enough. I want forever."

* * * *

Annie breathed in Colin's intoxicating fresh scent as she relaxed against him. "Forever sounds wonderful. A bed even more so."

"Then we need to return to Holyrood." He kissed her softly as he straightened her skirts.

"I cannae wait to join fully with you." The brilliant golden depths of his eyes and the love she saw reflected back at her, touched her soul. She stroked his chest. "I'm sorry for making you ride out here after me. I should never have left my chamber."

"Aye, and you should have alerted the guards when given the chance."

"I couldnae let Hugh speak out against you. 'Twas your life on the line." She kissed his cheek. "How come you didnae free your chief? What went wrong?"

"When we arrived at Lachlan's cell, he told us he'd received an offer, one he couldnae turn down. For his agreement, the king intends to look into the return of his lands on Islay."

"You mean the Rhinns?"

"Aye, the ownership of that piece of land has been in dispute for many years. Lachlan also informed us the MacDonalds had been removed from the cells and locked in a secure chamber in the palace. They've agreed to the king's demands."

"That does no' explain why you remained?"

"'Tis doubtful the guards will be able to identify us." He

kissed the tip of her nose. "You disabled three of them."

"No' the last one."

"The remaining guard held Lachlan captive, but Lachlan called us Malcolm and Munro, and with our masks in place and our identities hidden, there's no reason why we couldnae remain."

"There's still a risk."

"A small one, and a risk I was prepared to take to remain with you." He breathed out, long and deep. "Although Rory is now aware of what happened."

"And Hugh."

"Hugh's words will no' hold much sway considering your kidnapping."

"There's still a risk if you return, even if only a slight one. You and Arthur should continue onto Duart."

"I cannae leave you now, and dinnae ask it of me." Arms wrapped around her, he lifted his knees and kept her securely imprisoned against his chest. "No' when you have a terrible tendency to find trouble."

"I fear trouble is my middle name. You may well come to regret marrying me."

"My only regret will be that I didnae marry you sooner." His husky words held a world of promise and lightened her heart. "Do you intend to be a biddable wife now?"

"Aye, very biddable." She twined her arms around his neck. "Whatever you ask, I shall do."

"I'll hold you to that promise." He nibbled her lower lip then sucked it into his mouth. "I want you naked underneath me."

"Aye, please." She wriggled as tingles raced through her body. "I cannae believe we're in the middle of the forest, and so far from a chamber with a locked door."

"That is your fault." He chuckled and kissed her again.

"'Tis also a mistake I need to rectify."

"Good." He eased to his feet and set her down on hers. "We need to return, but first we need to break our fast. Are you hungry?"

"Very. Oh, and I forgot to tend to your injury." She smiled as she kissed his bruised chin. "Now, no more nicks and scratches for you."

"Aye, I'll do what I can." He threaded his fingers through hers and guided her back down the trail toward the burn.

At the edge of the meadow dotted with yellow flowers, Hugh stood roped to a large ash tree, and two feet above his head, one of the warriors had slapped a mound of moss into the trunk's crook.

Rory stood fifty feet back, his feet planted wide as he held his bow and arrow. He smiled at her. "Come here, Annie. You've been asking me to teach you how to shoot an arrow for years, and now you may have your chance. I've even set the target for you."

Naughty Rory. At Dunvegan, she'd trained twice a week under Rory's guidance on the archery field, although it had been Colin who'd first taught her to hunt with the bow from Mull's treetops while they'd sat on the wooden platform of his tree hut.

She wandered past a crackling fire where a warrior had skinned a small creature and now skewered meat onto sturdy sticks to prop onto a rack to cook. "Are you certain now is the right time to learn, Rory?"

"I'm certain, and 'tis a fine morning with the sun in the perfect position to highlight your target."

Aye, the sun's rays glimmered across the sparkling waters of the stream where one of her kinsmen filled several skins with water and plugged the tops. "All right, but I'll need a smaller bow. Yours looks far too big for me to hold."

"Jeremy," he called to his squire, a lad of sixteen who'd grown immensely of late. "Bring your bow."

Jeremy jogged across from the tethered horses, swung his

bow from his back and passed it to her.

"Thank you." She stepped in beside Rory. "Show me what to do, cousin."

"Set your feet apart and prepare the arrow."

"Like this?" She eased her right foot slightly in front of the left then slid the arrow into the notch. "Do I aim for the moss?"

"Aye, and the arrow needs to arch afore hitting its target, so allow for a higher degree of aim." He guided her hands to the right angle. "That should do."

There wasn't a chance she'd hit the target, not when her arrow was directed right at Hugh's head. She barely held back her giggle. "I see."

Hugh gritted his teeth.

"Nay, Rory. I think her aim is too high for this distance." Colin nudged Rory out of the way and with his arms around her from behind, pushed the tip of her arrow lower. "There, that's better."

She smothered her gasp. Now her arrow was on a direct target for Hugh's crotch.

"I cannae believe I'm about to get shot by a woman," Hugh grumbled as he squeezed his legs together.

"You willnae if she can maintain her focus," Colin admonished.

"Well, I'm very tired since I was forced to ride through the night, so my focus isnae quite what it should be." She placed her cheek to the side of the arrow as she pulled the bowstring back. At the last moment, she lifted the arrow tip and let it go. It flew free and arched perfectly as it sailed.

Hugh slammed his eyes shut, and she bounced onto her toes as she followed the arrow's path. The shaft speared the moss dead center.

"You have too much of a conscience," Colin grumbled as he strode to his horse and unstrapped his bow from his saddlebags. He returned to her side and readied his bow. "Let me show you how to take the perfect shot, scamp."

"Let's make that a double-perfect shot." Rory smiled as he stood next to Colin and took his position, his bow raised as they both lined up their sights. "Retribution can be sweet."

Colin's arrow sailed free first and thumped into the small V of wood between Hugh's legs, then a second later, Rory's arrow struck a hair's breadth above Hugh's head.

The warrior groaned. "Death may have been more kind than this torture."

"Death is too easy for you." Colin tapped his bottom lip as if considering where next to aim. After pulling another arrow from his pouch, he set it in place then released his shaft. It flew and splintered Rory's arrow in two.

"Nice." Rory readied for another strike. "Allow me to return the favor."

"Please do."

Rory's arrow speared Colin's shaft and Hugh hissed in pain. "Have mercy. A man needs his balls."

"Ah, but if you didnae have them, I'd be a happier man." Colin prepared his next shot. "As yet I've no' heard you apologize to my wife. 'Tis what I'm waiting for."

"Aye, I meant to." Hugh glanced at her. "My lady, I never should have taken you from your kin. Please, would you forgive me?"

"Your actions will never be forgiven." She rubbed her cheek against Colin's arm. "Not when you raised a sword against my husband."

"Good answer, scamp." Colin released his arrow. It landed a whisper from Hugh's ear with a thunk.

Rory tossed Colin another arrow. "I'd like to see you match that on the other side."

"W-wait." Hugh gulped in a breath. "I give you my word I'll never attempt such a misdeed again, no' against any woman."

"That's better, much better." Colin handed Rory back his arrow. "Excuse me. I have to feed my wife. Feel free to continue without me." He steered Annie toward the fire and spread out a tartan blanket one of the warriors had left there.

She sat and breathed in the succulent meaty aroma wafting toward her as across the river, the sun rose higher over the treetops and bathed them in its late autumn warmth. 'Twas beautiful this part of Scotland, but she missed the Western Isles, the crashing of the ocean's waves, the squawking seagulls, and children's giggles as they played along the beach. The isles were stunning with their glistening lochs and bens and moors.

Colin settled in behind her, his legs either side of hers. "What are you thinking that has that wistful look on your face?"

"I long for home."

"Soon, but no' yet." He tugged her back until she rested against his chest. Gently, he twined a lock of her hair around his finger, his warmth fully enclosing her. "You have the most beautiful hair. 'Tis so pale it shines like liquid gold."

"It does?"

"Aye, and I want to see it lying across my pillow every night." He selected one of the sticks of meat, tore off a chunk and slipped the morsel between her lips.

"That could be arranged." She plucked a piece of meat from the skewer and fed him.

In silence they ate as the other warriors wandered across and grabbed some food. A few men remained close to the fire and others strolled down to the stream.

Near the horses, Rory stowed his bow and arrow then ambled across. He perched on a low boulder after choosing a skewer and glanced at her. "We'll need to leave soon. Do you feel up to the ride?"

"Aye, I'm fine, and I dinnae care to leave Elizabeth worrying for too long."

"Then we'll leave once we've eaten."

Colin slid her hair over her shoulder and dropped a soft kiss on her neck.

Frowning, Rory eyed Colin and she eased across and blocked his view of her man.

Rory tapped his foot. "Annie, Colin can fight his own battles."

"Aye, but my wife is too protective by far," Colin rumbled over the top of her head.

"If I'm too protective, 'tis for a very good reason." She nodded at Rory. "You've looked after me for three years and for that I'll be forever grateful, but I've chosen the man I wish to spend my life with."

"Aye, so I've seen, although you'll always have my protection, whether you ask for it or no'." Rory chewed his meat. "You are more than a cousin to me. You are a sister in many ways."

She touched her heart. "And I consider you my brother."

"Sisters can also be rather annoying." A sly grin spread across his face as he stood. "Let's leave. 'Tis time to ride out." He kicked dirt over the fire and extinguished it, his decision to accept their relationship clearly made.

"Well, that went far better than I expected." She jumped to her feet and grasped Colin's hands. "I dinnae know what you were so worried about in speaking to Rory."

"Aye," he chuckled. "I've no idea." He stood and adjusted the front ties of her fur cloak, ensuring it was well secured for the ride.

Across the meadow, two MacLeod warriors slung Hugh and Fergus belly-down across their mounts' saddles. Their return ride wouldn't be pleasant, but at least they had their lives.

She crossed to Colin's destrier and he boosted her up then slid in behind her. With his arms around her waist, he grasped the reins and nudged his horse to follow the rest of their party.

With her hands on his black leather clad thighs, she relaxed into the ride as they galloped through the forest and across the grassy moors. Birds chirped high above the rolling fields of heather, and she smiled as Colin sang a gentle tune. 'Twas a Scottish song of bens and burns and of the hearth and home, one she knew well. "It's been an age since I've heard that. My mother used to sing it all the time when she pottered around her kitchen."

"That's where I learnt it." He rubbed his chin over the top of her head.

"I remember those days as if they were yesterday. You used to sit at the table next to your mother when you visited. You'd no' move until the oatcakes had cooled, then you'd pinch the biggest one afore I could get my hands on it."

"You didnae need the biggest one when you were so little," he whispered in her ear.

"And you were too big to argue the point with."

"I still am."

"Aye, but I like how big you are now." She half-turned and grinned at him. The wind whipped his dark shoulder-length hair behind him, the blond tipped ends adding a rakish look she completely adored. "Hopefully you willnae argue with me quite so often anymore."

"I highly doubt that, unless you suddenly learn how to follow my orders."

"Orders can be wearying." She yawned and patted her mouth. The long hours of riding through the night had caught up with her and she was so comfortable.

"Rest if you need to."

"Nay, I wish to talk with you some more." Still, she closed her eyes and snuggled against him. Calm descended and she slowly drifted, the man she loved at her back and the future she'd always longed for within her reach.

He was the air she breathed and the man she lived for.

* * * *

Holding Annie safe and close in his arms brought such peace to Colin's soul. The destination he rode toward though did not. He too would have preferred to continue on to Mull, but that option wasn't possible with Ian and Murdock still awaiting his arrival at the faerie stones.

Night descended, the sun dipping below the horizon and sending a final flare of red across the sky. It bathed the palace in a fiery glow as they neared.

Annie stirred, blinked her eyes open and smiled at him. "We're back already?"

"Aye." He trotted through Holyrood's gates and pulled his horse to a stop outside the stables. "You clearly needed the rest."

"Annie!" Elizabeth hurried across the courtyard in a flurry of forest green skirts, the loose wisps of her auburn hair having escaped her high top knot fluttering around her face.

He dismounted and swung Annie down beside him. "I will see you inside, soon. Go with your aunt."

"Are you sure?"

"That's an order."

"All right. Be careful." She kissed his cheek then raced toward her aunt. The two women embraced with an excited squeal then Elizabeth steered Annie inside.

He handed his horse's reins to the stable hand as across the bailey, the captain of the king's guard strode toward them in his finely cut uniform.

The man tugged the dark cuffs of his coat as he passed his narrowed gaze over the restrained MacDonalds still slung over their saddles. He stopped in front of him and Rory. "'Tis good to see you've captured the men who kidnapped your ward, although there is only two. What happened to the rest of the MacDonald warriors?"

"They refused to submit in battle, and 'twas either their lives or ours." Rory motioned toward Hugh and Fergus. "I'd appreciate it if you ensured they remain in your cells until the king decides their fate."

"I'll see to it immediately." The captain gestured for one of his men to take the MacDonalds. "Unfortunately the king left no' long after you did. There's unrest at the borders that demanded his immediate attention."

"What of the three chiefs?" Rory asked. "Has the king concluded his negotiations with Lachlan MacLean and Donald and Angus MacDonald?"

"I'm afraid those talks have gone on hold until the king returns."

"Is Lachlan still in the tower?" Colin asked the king's captain.

"He now resides in a locked chamber in the main palace, although under heavy guard as the MacDonalds do." His gaze narrowed. "Are you aware an attempt to free your chief was made at midnight during the ball's unmasking?"

"My ward was abducted around that time and I was rather busy riding across the country."

"Three of the tower guardsmen were disabled with spiked ale a maid brought them." He palmed the hilt of his sword, suspicion clouding his gaze. "The remaining guard identified the assailants as Malcolm and Munroe MacLean. Do you know of them?"

"I've no' seen them since I left Duart. I wasnae even aware they'd traveled to Edinburgh."

"The gate guardsmen also confirmed two warriors wearing MacLean plaids rode out no' long after midnight, mayhap a half hour afore you and your party did."

"Then that must have been the culprits." Ian and Murdock had done their job in diverting suspicion from him and Arthur. Thank heavens.

Arms crossed, Rory glared at the captain. "Colin was also with me at the time of the unmasking, right afore we spent the rest of the night chasing Hugh MacDonald."

"Then I apologize, but of course I had to ask." The captain nodded at them both. "I wouldnae be doing my duty otherwise."

"Then you've asked, but now allow us on our way." Rory slanted his head. "Unless you have other urgent business you need to speak of."

"There is none. I bid you both a good night." The captain joined his guardsman and together they both hauled Hugh and Fergus away.

"Thank you." Colin clapped Rory on the back.

"I cannae have you behind bars. That would cause Annie distress, something I'd never tolerate." He clasped Colin's forearms. "Look after her. She holds a special place in my heart, just as her parents did."

"I give you my word that I'll guard her with my life."

"Then I'll also have your promise you'll bring her home to Dunvegan for the Twelfth Night and Yule celebrations. Elizabeth and my sister will never forgive me if she's no' there."

"We'll come." He grinned and stepped back. "Rest well, Rory."

"Aye, you too."

He would only rest once Annie was back in his arms.

Hurrying, he collected his belongings from his chamber and strode to Annie's room. 'Twas time to court his wife, and make her his in every way.

Chapter 8

"I'm sorry you've been so worried, Elizabeth." Annie paced her chamber, wishing she hadn't left Colin. 'Twas too soon to have him out of her sight after all she'd gone through.

"I cannae believe Hugh MacDonald's nerve. That man deserves all that is coming to him." Elizabeth stepped in front of her, her voice harsh but still a whisper with her maid in the room. "What did he want from you?"

"He intended to force my hand, to take me as his wife once we reached Dunscaith." She shuddered and rubbed her cold hands together.

"Despicable man." She pulled her into another hug and patted her back. "We'll have you warm soon enough, my dear."

At a knock on the door, Maggie rose from where she stoked the fire, dusted her hands on her white aproned skirts and opened the door. A servant entered with a tray and set it on the side table while two barefoot lads with sooty imprints on the knees of their breeches heaved a tub in and set it before the hearth. They all left along with her maid to fetch the water.

"Sit." Elizabeth pulled out a chair. "Warm food in your belly will be good for you."

For Elizabeth's sake, she selected a morsel of salmon and

took a bite. The roasted potato and seasoned vegetables looked delicious, but she couldn't manage them when her belly was still in revolt with worry for Colin. She pushed the plate away. "I'll eat more once Colin is here."

"He'll be fine." Elizabeth's gaze softened. "I've heard the two men who attempted to free Lachlan were sighted riding out afore Colin and Rory took off in pursuit of you. They wore MacLean plaids."

"Oh, you should have said sooner. That is good news." Ian and Murdock must have provided an alibi for Colin and Arthur. "I wonder if Colin knows?"

"If he does no', then he will soon enough."

At another knock, Elizabeth opened the door and the maids returned along with the lads, each carrying a steaming pail of water. They filled the tub, and heat pulsed through the room. "We'll let you bathe and rest." Elizabeth squeezed her hands. "I'll see you in the morn."

"Aye, in the morn." She shut the door after they all filed out, her troubled thoughts more at ease after hearing Elizabeth's news.

Perhaps a bath would relax her further. She tugged her riding boots and stockings off then quickly shed her clothes and sank into the glorious water. 'Twas wonderful and warmed her through. She dunked her head and when she came up, Colin stood inside the room, his molten gold gaze roaming over her.

"You're free?"

"Ian and Murdock ensured that, as well as Rory who just vouched for me."

"And Hugh and Fergus?"

"In the cells."

"Then all is well?" She eased back against the rim, her breasts bobbing along the surface.

"Aye, although I'm feeling rather achy." He knelt at the tub's edge, cupped one of her breasts and stroked the pebbled tip. "I'm hungry."

"There's food on the table."

"Nay, my love, 'tis you holds the feast I need, and I cannae stay here while you're in there." He kicked off his boots and removed his padded cotun and tunic. His tanned chest and rippling abs gleamed under the dancing firelight.

"I've never bathed with a man afore." She squirmed back against the rim to make more room for him.

"I should hope no', otherwise we'll need to have words." He lifted a brow as he gripped the waistband of his leather trews. A delicious tease of dark hair narrowed down his rigid belly and disappeared below. Now she hungered too, every inch of her.

"Mmm, watching you undress is a pleasure all unto itself."

"Then I best no' disappoint you." He shoved his black trews down his thickly muscled thighs and stepped out of them. His cock bobbed free and brushed his belly, rigid and hard and all hers. Sloshing the water, he stepped in and eased down. His gaze smoldered as he nabbed the soap and lathered it. "What would you like me to clean first? Your ticklish toes?"

"If you touch my toes, I'll kick you." She'd been six and he twelve when he'd first discovered how ticklish she was there. One summer's day when he'd been aiding her into the saddle, his fingers had slid between her bare toes and she'd squealed and jumped so high, she'd flown right over her horse and landed on the hard ground instead. He'd raced around to check on her, but seeing she was fine, had grinned and begun tickling her in earnest. She'd laughed so hard until tears had streamed from her eyes.

"Mayhap later then. I like hearing your giggles." He lifted her feet over his shoulders then nabbed the soap and stroked her calves and inner thighs until bubbles abounded.

She sank back, her head against the rim and her blond hair swirling around her. His hands smoothed over her hips and along her back, his touch so decadently delicious.

"Annie," he whispered, his heated gaze on hers. "You're so beautiful. I cannae believe you're all mine."

"As you're all mine."

"And I always will be." He swished her hair away from her breasts and caressed them.

"Never stop touching me." A fiery tingle radiated from the sensitive tips.

"I never intend to." With his hands on her sides, he lifted her out of the water and sat her astride his hips. He trailed kisses along her jaw and neck then trailed down and licked her nipples, first one and then the other.

"I need to touch you too." She reached under the water, skimmed her fingers along his cock and stroked him in long pulls, eager to give him the same pleasure he gave her.

"Too much," he groaned. "I'll never be able hold on if you do that."

"Aye, but that's what I want, for you no' to hold on." She nuzzled his neck, drew the soft skin deep inside her mouth and sucked as she pumped him harder.

"Oh hell." He shifted restlessly underneath her. "That feels so good. You have magical hands and a magical mouth." He dipped one finger through her curls and caressed her clit.

She moved up onto her knees and guided his cock to her folds. Using his plump head, she massaged it along her entrance, back and forth until she wriggled and squirmed for more. "What do I do?"

"We need a bed." He wrapped his arms around her, rose out of the tub and carried her to the mattress. With their wet bodies sliding together, he laid her down on the soft brown fur and took her mouth in a ravenous kiss.

Goodness. He was hard, very hard, and nothing separated them any longer. Not the danger of Colin freeing his chief or a MacDonald intent on kidnap. She wound her fingers into his dark locks and pushed her hips toward him. "Show me what it's like to join as one."

"They'll be a pinch of pain, but I'll bring you pleasure afore that happens." He looked into her eyes as he plunged one finger deep inside her. He kissed her and she bucked as he stroked, harder and faster until he curled his finger into a spot that had her arching for more.

She rocked against him, her pulse jumping out of rhythm as desire and need bolted through her. Aye, pleasure. He always gave her pleasure.

* * * *

Colin had longed for Annie every moment of their separation, to join with her and make her his in every way. Now her soft moans were driving every rational thought from his head. Kissing her, tasting the delectable recesses of her mouth had his cock throbbing for release.

Still stroking her below, he slid down her body. He traced her skin with his mouth and tongue, gorged himself on her full breasts and sucked her pebbled nipples until she cried out for more.

"I want to make you come, Annie, over and over until you cannae breathe for the pleasure." He feasted on her creamy flesh as he glided down to her entrance where he longed to taste her.

Blood pounding, he lowered his head to her clit and razzed the tip with his teeth. She was his, always his, and his mind went dark with lust as he smoothed his hands along her inner thighs and opened her up more fully for his touch. He drank her in, allowing his desperate need for her to consume him.

"I have to touch you too." With the softest caress, she stroked his shaft, her thumb swiping seductively over the head, and his cock pounded at him to take her.

"Annie, have mercy."

"Nay, I want you, now."

Aye, he couldn't hold on any longer. With his hands on her hips, he lifted her to him and moved between her legs. He teased his cock along her slick folds and then covering her mouth with his, kissed her until she arched into him.

"I love you." He pushed against her thin barrier, tore through her innocence and plunged deep inside her.

"Oh." She sighed into his mouth, clutched his butt and pulled him in even deeper. "You feel so good, like there isnae an inch of me no' filled with you."

"Aye, we are one." He lifted up then slowly pushed back in. "From this day forth."

She kissed him and he pounded harder and deeper.

His thoughts flew as she raked his back and cried his name. Then he was lost as her inner muscles tightened and dragged him in. He roared, his release exploding violently along with hers as he spilled his seed deep within her.

'Twas a perfect union, as if his soul had locked tight with hers for all time.

"My wife," he whispered as he kissed her again. "I will never let you go."

* * * *

Annie stretched on the fur covers then jerked as something tickled her feet. "Colin," she growled, still half asleep even though bright morning sunshine beamed into her chamber. "Stop right there."

At the end of her bed, he stood with a grin on his face. "You are so easy to tease."

"You're naked and holding a tray."

"Aye, but I didnae leave here to fetch this without clothing. You didnae even hear me return." He strolled around the bed, set the tray on the mattress between them then sprawled on his side and faced her. From between two slices of apple pastry and cream, he plucked a white rose free and passed it to her. "For you."

"'Tis beautiful." She breathed the sweetly perfumed fragrance in.

"I snuck out to the king's garden then on my way back, begged the cook for a treat. I know how you adore your apple pastry." He leaned in and kissed her bare shoulder, his cock twitching and lengthening as he did.

"It looks delicious." She chose one of the pastry slices and bit into it. So sweet. She gobbled another mouthful and the cream on top oozed and plopped onto her chest.

"Wait. Allow me." He shifted the tray to one side, cupped her breasts and gently licked her flesh.

"Stop pinching my food."

"When it lands on you, 'tis mine." He swiped his finger through the cream on the other pastry and smeared a line from her breasts to her belly. "And this is how I prefer to eat mine."

"Colin, you cannae do that." He stretched over top of her and her heartbeat raced.

"Oh, I assure you, I can." After kissing along the trail, he dipped his tongue around her belly button and drifted lower. With her legs spread, he settled between then then coated her clit with another swipe of cream. The cool delicacy melted against her hot flesh.

She squeezed her eyes shut as he suckled and probed with his tongue and sent a wave of intense sensations thrumming through her. "I never knew you could be so wicked."

"Only with you," he rumbled as he feasted.

"That feels so good." Desire pooled and every flick of his tongue over her nub built her orgasm higher. Such torture, yet of the most exquisite kind. "Come inside me. I want to be filled with you."

"'Tis best we wait until you heal. You must be sore."

"It will hurt more if you wait." She pushed him onto his back and rolled on top of him, and as his cock pressed hard and heavy between them, she kissed him back.

"You're still no' taking orders very well, love."

"What order?" She rubbed the hard tips of her breasts over

his chest and sighed with delight as they tingled against his crisp hair. Still, it wasn't enough. Needing more, she wriggled down his body. "I itch to kiss you as you've kissed me."

Gently, she palmed his balls and caressed the smooth skin. His cock strained and bobbed closer to her mouth and she dipped her head and swirled her tongue over him.

"Oh hell." He caught her face and kept her in place as he arched into her. "I've dreamed of you taking me in your mouth again."

"Mmm, as have I." She settled her lips over the top of his cock and took him deep. With long pulls, she sucked him, teasing him from root to tip.

"Annie," he croaked. "I need you to take me inside you. I dinnae wish to come in your pretty mouth." He dragged her up, spread his hands over her hips and lifted her over his shaft. "Sit on me."

"Aye, that I would like." She rubbed his slick head over her clit then slid him between her wet folds. Slowly, inch by inch, she lowered and seated herself fully on top of him. Her channel tightened as even more need poured through her. "What do I do now?"

"Ride me." His golden eyes twinkled. "And whatever else takes your fancy."

"Like on a great stallion?" She eased up then sank back down, taking his cock deep into the heart of her. She moaned at the sweet sensation. "Oh, I'm about to reap the reward from all my faithful years of riding across every terrain."

"It does no' hurt?"

"No' one bit." She leaned forward, her hands either side of his face as she rocked back and forth, faster and faster until the pressure built to a crescendo in her core.

"That's it. Come as you please. I'm right here with you." He caught her bobbing breasts between his lips and drew one nipple deep inside his mouth. The tension of need within her wound tighter, and with one decisive flick of his finger over her clit, he sent her soaring from her body.

Writhing, she gave into the whirlpool of emotions taking her. She convulsed around him, crying out his name as she flew, and as she rode the waves, he rolled her onto her back and sank balls-deep inside her with a fierce groan.

"You hold my heart in your hands, Annie." He moved gently inside her, so tenderly bringing them both back down. "You have ever since the day you were born. I was there that day. I waited with my father and yours as your mother brought you into this world, and when I heard your first cry, I snuck into her chamber and to my mother's side as she aided the midwife. You were swaddled in white cloth, your big blue eyes wide open and sweet dimples showing either side of your tiny mouth."

Tears misted her gaze. "You've never told me that afore."

"There are many things I've yet to tell you. You were the girl who captivated me as a lad, and now the woman who's owns my heart. I will always be wherever you are."

"And I will always be wherever you are." She kissed him and allowed his words to sink deep inside her heart.

They'd been together from the very beginning, and they'd be together until the very end.

He was the one man she could never live without.

Chapter 9

Later that night, the last thing Colin wanted to do was leave the warmth of Annie's arms and ride out to the faerie stones, but no more could he delay. Ian and Murdock would be waiting for word of their chief and what had transpired since the masquerade. If he didn't go soon, they might well try to come to him.

He shoved his feet over the side of the bed, opened his traveling satchel and pulled out clean leather trews. With his fur vest donned over his tunic to ward off the night's chill, he slid his sword belt on and sheathed his wrist daggers.

Taking care not to wake Annie, he pressed a gentle kiss to her forehead and whispered, "I'll be back soon."

At the door, he took one last look and with her sensual image entrenched in his mind, he slipped out of the room and strode to Arthur's chamber.

He knocked and his man opened the door already dressed for a ride in his tan leather jerkin and boots. "Ian and Murdock will be waiting."

"Aye, I expected you. I hope the garrison guards will no' wonder why we're riding out so late, and mere hours after we've returned." He closed the door and they headed to the stables.

"Then we'll ride first toward the city. It isnae unusual for a warrior to enjoy a night at the establishments open at such a late hour. Look eager." He couldn't have suspicions being raised now he'd ensured his innocence.

Arthur mounted and then leaning closer, said, "You'll have to hope Annie does no' hear about your sudden penchant for the night life."

"She has more trust in me than that." With an exuberant hoot, he galloped through the gates with Arthur at his side. He also intended to be back well afore she awoke, and he would gladly convince her then of how very much he longed only for her.

Once they'd cleared the guardsmen's sight, they changed course and veered into the forest. The trail they followed that lead up into the hills was the same route that led toward The King's Tavern where he'd collected Annie from, although the faerie stones were slightly off to the south east. Damn. James. He'd left without thinking to check if MacDonald had returned to the palace in the hours since he and Annie had.

"You look worried," Arthur called as he pounded next to him.

"Have you heard if James MacDonald has recovered from his chest illness?"

"I didnae see him during the evening meal in the great hall, but aye, word is he's returned."

"Then 'tis best we find Ian and Murdock then leave as soon as we can." Urging his destrier to a faster pace, he bolted out of the darkened forest and along a grassy ridge bathed in the moon's glow. He rode hard until the mystical stone circle appeared.

The massive slabs of stone shone a ghostly white in the dark of night, a clear warning to all to keep a respectful distance, and there, tucked in a hollow near the trees just beyond, a fire flickered.

Ian and Murdock rose to their feet and signaled them all was well.

Colin slowed his horse, pulled up and dismounted. He slung his reins over a low branch and grasped his clansmen's forearms. "'Tis good to see you both made it safely away from the palace."

"We ensured our MacLean plaids were seen, except no alarm was raised and none of the guards followed us." Ian motioned for him to sit. "Warm yourself afore the fire. We're eager to hear news of Lachlan."

Colin eased down onto a squat stone and stretched his legs toward the fire's heat. "The chief's been removed from the tower and now resides in a heavily guarded chamber in the palace, although negotiations have gone on hold while the king deals with a skirmish at the borders.

"What of your return to the great hall? It must have gone well for you to be here." Ian perched on a log next to Murdock while Arthur picked up the wooden pail propped against the tree and set it before their horses. Their mounts lapped the water.

"It went well, but soon after we returned, we discovered Annie had gone missing and that Hugh MacDonald had abducted her. The man was waiting for the prime opportunity to take her, and the moment it presented itself, he did."

"You caught him up?" Ian picked up a stick and prodded the burning embers.

"Aye, and the MacDonalds have been dealt with. Hugh was tossed into the cells and now awaits the king's punishment. Annie is safe, and in the morn, the four of us will be escorting her back to Duart. I need her where she can no longer find trouble."

"You dinnae wish for Murdock and I to stay?"

"Nay, the king's men are well aware they're searching for two of our clansmen, and though you are no' known as Malcolm and Munroe, if they find you, they may well decide your presence here in the city is proof enough to throw you into the cells. I also need your sword arm on the journey back to Duart. I want my wife to have our full protection."

"Your wife?" Ian cocked a brow. "About time. My congratulations."

"You have mine too," Murdock added with a grin. "That is one union we need to celebrate."

"Which we will, on our return to MacLean land." Colin stood. "We leave immediately."

Aye, the sooner he had Annie back behind Duart's walls, the sooner he'd be able to breathe without his fear for her his constant companion.

* * * *

Colin was gone? Annie dressed and hurried into the great hall in the hopes of finding him amongst those breaking their fast. His side of the mattress had been stone cold, as if he'd left her bed some hours before, but that couldn't be. He wouldn't leave without first speaking to her.

She entered the great hall and searched the crowded room. A feast had been laid out and the trestle tables overflowed with platters of cooked meat, boiled eggs and bread. She sidestepped around the perimeter, hands clasped in her sapphire skirts, but Colin was nowhere to be seen.

"Annie, there you are." James strode toward her, looking hearty and hale in tan breeches and a rich brown silk doublet over a white tunic, his red hair a mass of unruly curls.

"James, you look well. When did you return?"

"Late last eve, although I've heard gossip this morn which we need to speak about." He extended his arm. "I need a word in private."

"Of course." She took his arm. "Mayhap outside?"

"Aye, after being stuck indoors for days, I could use the fresh air." He guided her through the balcony doors, down the short flight of stairs and along the stone path surrounded by thick lavender bushes. "There is much we need to speak about."

"Did you hear about my news?" A gust blew and made her hair tickle her face.

He tucked the strands behind her ear. "If you're speaking of Hugh and his abduction, then my men informed me. I dinnae condone his actions, but Hugh has been reckless of late, particularly since his wife's death." He walked toward a rose arbor with a wooden slatted seat underneath it and motioned for her to sit. "I also heard you'd spoken handfast vows with Colin MacLean. Tell me that isnae true."

"'Tis true." She sat and faced him, her hands folded in her lap. "Which means I'm sure you'll understand why I must say nay to your proposal."

"The MacLeans of Duart are trouble and Colin MacLean more than any of them." Looking into her eyes, he took her hands in his callused ones. "Annie, a handfast isnae as binding as a marriage and the vows can easily be broken. Did you speak them for fear of what had happened between us? That you remained unchaperoned at the tavern?"

"I was worried rumors would surface, but that's no' the reason I bound myself to Colin."

"I'd never have spoken against you." His gaze pleaded her understanding. "I'm naught like my cousin, and my offer still stands. Is there any possibility you might be persuaded to join with me? Together we could form an unwavering alliance."

"You were kind to me while I stayed at Dunscaith, and for that I'll always be grateful, but I am very happy with the man I've chosen." Or she would be if she could find him.

"I fear you've made your decision too fast. I certainly wasnae given the opportunity to—"

"James MacDonald!" Colin, his face thunderously dark, stormed down the path. "Get your hands off my wife."

"Colin, nay. It isnae as it seems." She dived between the men as they came at each other and shoved one hand against each of their heaving chests.

"He was touching you, Annie." Colin swung her in behind him, raised his sword and glared at James. "What is it with you MacDonalds that you cannae leave what's no' yours alone?"

"You cannae speak. She's your ward, and now you've taken advantage of her."

"Please, let's discuss this like rational adults." She gripped Colin's sword arm, his very immoveable sword arm. Oh goodness. He had to listen to her. "Colin, put your weapon down. James means neither of us any harm. He does no' even raise his blade."

James grunted and eyed her. "You truly care for him?"

"With all my heart." She smiled even in the tense moment. "I'm so sorry, James. The only man I ever wish to wed is the one you see afore you."

"Damn it," James grumbled, his palm firm on his belted sword hilt.

"James, I'm most grateful for your friendship, but that's all I'll ever seek from you. Please, I hope you can understand."

"What of Anne? She longs to see you. She's your kin."

"I long to see her too. She's like the sister I never had, and I hope in the future I can safely visit with her. Certainly we could meet at Dunvegan since the next Highland Games are to be held there. Do you and your brother intend to go?"

"Alex and I would never miss the chance to challenge the other clans, and aye, the games will be a safe place to meet. Anne has certainly never experienced the festivities and talks about it constantly. Her MacLeod kin hold a special place in her heart."

"Then I'll see her there." Relief poured through her and she sniffed and wiped a trickling tear from her cheek. "Even with all that's happened these past days, there is still hope that in the future you and Alex, and Anne and I will be able to work on restoring some form of bond between the clans. Colin too once I persuade him. I miss Anne. Tell her I'm now as happy as she is.

That I've found the man I've always wished for. She'll understand what I mean."

"I'll pass on your words."

"Thank you." She squeezed James's hands then stepped back and nestled against Colin's side. "I consider you a friend, James, and I always will."

"I wished for more, but since you've clearly made your choice, you have my good wishes." He turned his gaze on Colin. "My brother and I are heartily sick of this feud, whether you wish to believe that or no'. Unfortunately, my cousin's recent actions may have set the path to peace back between us, but understand this, his opinions are his alone."

Colin eyed James, rather skeptically. "If you truly wish for peace, then in the future, leave my wife out of your pursuits." He sheathed his sword. "And when we meet at the Games, mayhap we'll actually enjoy some friendly rivalry."

"I look forward to coming up against you." James nodded at her. "Farewell, Annie." He walked away.

"Leaving you alone is dangerous." Colin tipped up her chin, his molten gaze burning. "That shall no' happen again for a very long time."

"Well, that I heartily agree to." She arched into him, enjoying every moment of his undivided attention. "I believe I hear our bed calling. Do you heartily agree to us returning there?"

"I prefer my bed on Mull, and I cannae wait to get you there." He swung her into his arms and kissed her. "You're my destiny, Annie. You always have been."

"As you're mine." She cradled his face in her hands. "I love you, and only you."

Oh aye, their destiny had bound them together from the very beginning, and it would throughout all time.

Chapter 10

On the narrow wooden platform edging Colin's childhood tree hut, Annie knelt behind her warrior guardian and played her fingers in his dark wind-tossed hair. It had been a fortnight since their return to Duart, and within hours of their arrival, they'd spoken vows before Brother John and their entire clan. The robed clergyman had blessed their marriage and she'd never been so happy.

"I love this place," she murmured in his ear. "After you left it behind in your later years, I adored coming here." The forest rose all around, and before them, the glistening blue-green waters of the Sound of Mull rolled in and splashed over the rocky beach. Even the stormy weather of the past few days had finally cleared and now a cloudless sky beckoned a sultry blue.

"I never left it behind." He pushed the creaky door behind her open and toppled her inside onto the thick fur blankets they'd not long risen from. "Surely you've noticed it's never fallen into disrepair."

Aye, only one board on the seaside wall needed replacing. The wooden ceiling and floor remained solid and strong. "I should have known."

"There are too many good memories for me here, and now

we've made even more." He swept his hands underneath the tunic she'd swiped from him and caressed her bare bottom. "This place will be preserved for all time."

"I can think of another memory I'd like to make here since you seem intent on creating them." She skimmed her fingers across his tanned chest then tip-toed down to the loose ties of his leather trews.

"And what memory would that be, scamp?" His golden eyes heated to a smoldering hue.

"The memory of you giving me your babe."

"Then I willnae rest until I've done that." He stripped off her shirt and kissed her with such sweet seduction. "Ah, all mine."

Tingles raced across her skin and with breathless hunger she gave into the need to join with him.

Love.

It was timeless and could bloom from the day one was born.

"Aye, all yours," she whispered. "We'll be together, forever."

Author's Note

In the year fifteen-hundred and ninety, the blood feuds ran rampant between the Highlander clans of the Western Isles of Scotland. During this period, the king had imprisoned the three chiefs, Lachlan MacLean of Duart, Donald MacDonald of Sleat, and Angus MacDonald of Dunnyveg. He intended to bring a halt to the feud and for them to atone for their actions, and so as each chief arrived in Edinburgh at the king's request, they were apprehended and imprisoned. In each of the stand-alone books in this *Highlander Heat* series, you can catch the individual stories of the clans, and discover how the feud began and the ramifications of it as it raged.

Sir Lachlan Mor MacLean was the fourteenth Chief of Clan MacLean of Duart, and with his son, Hector Og MacLean, a minor at the time, I chose Colin MacLean and his brother to lead the clan.

Colin MacLean and Annie MacLeod are however fictional characters.

Sir Roderick Ruairidh Mor MacLeod, the fifteenth chief of clan MacLeod, was known as Rory and as stated in this story, was indeed favored by the king and had his ear.

This story is woven with as much accuracy to the period

and locations as possible, but any mistakes made are mine alone.

This book forms part of my *Highlander Heat* series, and each within it are stand-alone.

If you wish to read a little more about Annie, she first featured in Highlander's Castle, book one, while Colin played a pivotal role in Highlander's Charm, book three.

Please feel free to search for any of my other works. I simply adore strong heroines, and have a ton of fun matching them with their honorable alpha heroes.

**Also available in paperback
Scottish Historical Romance**

Traveling through time…for a Highlander.

Highlander Heat Series

Highlander's Castle, Book One

Highlander's Magic, Book Two

Highlander's Charm, Book Three

Highlander's Guardian, Book Four

Highlander's Faerie, Book Five

Highlander's Champion, Book Six

by Joanne Wadsworth

Looking for more sexy Scottish adventure?

Read on to catch a preview of the next book in the
Highlander Heat series.

Highlander's Faerie

Highlander Heat Book Five

by Joanne Wadsworth

Highlander's Faerie

Highlander Heat Series, Book Five

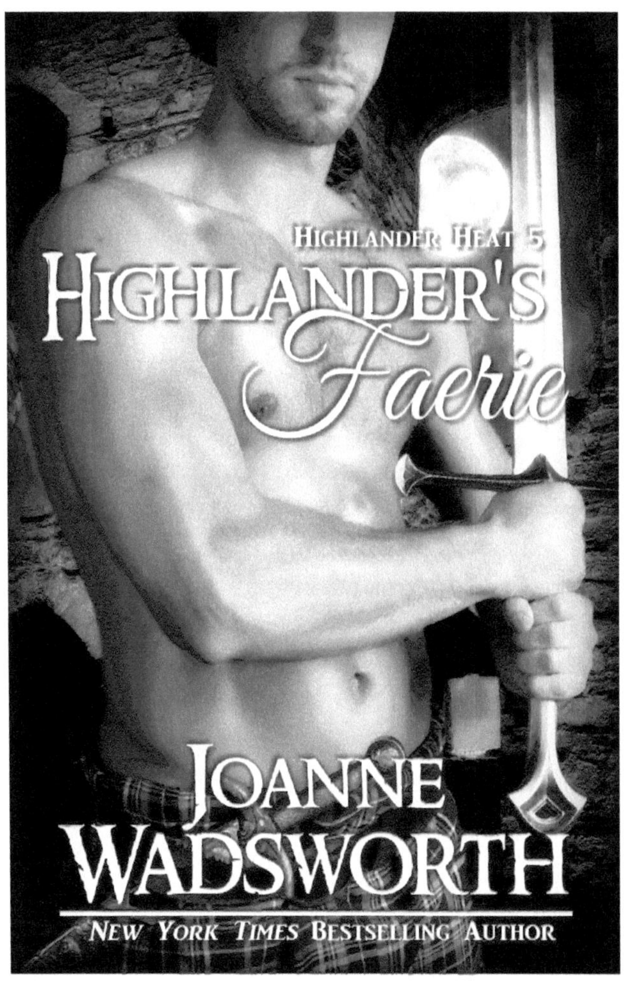

The Faerie Circle

The ruins of Dunyvaig Castle, on the Isle of Islay, Scotland, current day.

The full moon, a bright ball of eerie orange, hung low along the ocean's horizon and cast its glow over ghostly wisps of cloud floating across it. The wind rose, and inside Dunyvaig's faerie circle, Katherine MacLean huddled on the cold, damp grass, her knees drawn tight to her chest. Nine white stones standing six feet high and six feet apart surrounded her, while a tenth center stone, short enough to sit on but just as wide, shone marble smooth with her ancestor's silver amulet draped upon it. Mary's MacLean's talisman had been engraved on one side with the MacLean clan crest, and on the reverse, the MacDonald crest. The piece had been gifted to Mary on the day she'd wed the MacDonald chief, and should have represented the time when the two great clans had finally come together in harmony. Instead the feud had become bitterer and raged across the Western Isles.

Even as Mary's kin had battled, she'd continued to wear the amulet as a firm reminder she belonged to both clans, until the day had come when Mary had decided nothing more could be done except to ask the faerie folk for aid. She'd stood in this circle and made a wish, asking the Guardians of Dunyvaig to aid her in bringing peace between her clans. They'd instructed her to bequeath her amulet to her eldest daughter, requesting it be passed down through the generations until it once again came into the possession of the eldest daughter born to a MacLean. That had taken over four-hundred years, but it was a gift Katherine's older twin sister, Marie, had held dear to her heart.

Marie had received the bestowment on her twenty-first birthday, and following it, Katherine and Marie had traveled halfway around the world, from Australia's Gold Coast to Scotland's mainland then by ferry to this beautiful isle. As the progeny of two bickering clans, they'd brought Mary's amulet home as she'd requested.

Then a mere week ago, Katherine had stood in this faerie circle with her sister and made a wish that had gone awry. That wish had lowered the veil and taken Marie away from her and far into the past.

Behind Katherine, high on the craggy hill, Dunyvaig's ruins tormented her. Those blocks of jagged stone lay so heartbreakingly cold and alone, as she'd been this past week without her sister. Rocking, she allowed her tears to trickle free. "Please," she cried out to the little folk, "I'll do whatever you ask of me. Grant me one more wish. Allow me to join my sister. She's all I have left in this world."

Pain speared through her and she slumped onto her side. Blood flowed down her neck from an open wound that had come out of nowhere. She grasped the edges, but her lifeblood poured through her fingers and soaked her red and blue tartan coat.

Vision blurring, she scrambled to the edge of the circle and hit a hazy barrier. Beyond the fog, the darkened waves of Lagavulin Bay rolled in with a pounding crash, and high on the hill, Dunyvaig Castle rose strong. Three stories high, its battlements topped fortified walls and candles glowed from the tower windows.

"Mary, you're no' to wander beyond the gates," a guardsman bellowed as he rushed across the top of the barbican.

A woman with a riot of red-gold curls swaying around her belly swollen with child hurried toward the circle and patted the sides. "The veil has risen," Mary called to the guard. Kneeling in her white gown, she peered within, right at Katherine. Softly, she murmured, "Please, whose presence do I feel? That of the fae?"

"I need your aid." Katherine fought to get to her knees and hammered the veil with what strength she had.

"I hear whispers from within." Mary searched the circle. "Guardians of Dunyvaig, I implore you. Marie has gone to battle for the Rhinns and I fear for her safety. She will perish if my brother's life is taken. Lachlan MacLean has yet to father her paternal line. If he dies, she dies."

"Mary, you have to send someone to Marie." She clutched her wounded neck.

"Aye, if that is what the fae ask of me, then that is what I shall do."

"I'm not one of the—"

"Ye must come inside, Mary." The guard strode out in a thick fur vest and breeches, his sword at his side. "'Tis late and the weather turns."

"Nay, I need a moment. I can sense the fae's presence." Mary bowed her head against the veil. "Please, show yourself to me."

"There is none there. Now come." The warrior helped Mary to her feet and gently led her back through the gates.

"Mary, stay. I—I—" Black spots danced before her eyes. No. She had to hold on.

"Katherine." A voice floated all around and a light shimmered. "I am one of the fae and have heard your wish. If your desire is to join your sister then you must survive. Your paternal ancestor is wounded, just as you are. Hold strong."

"I need Marie." She fought the descending fog.

"I know. You've always needed each other." Another voice, and not one she'd ever forget, not when it belonged to her late mother. She blinked and forced her vision to clear. A glowing form made of mist and moonlight materialized and took the shape of the woman who'd given birth to her, the woman she'd mourned since her death only a few months past.

"Mum? Am I dead?"

"No, but I'm here. Your father and I never wished to leave you and I've always been close, as is he."

Another form shimmered to radiant life next to her mother.

"Dad?" On her knees, she tried to grab them but met nothing but air.

Thunder rumbled all around and lightning hit the rippling waves of the bay with a sizzling crackle. The veil thinned and her parents and the faerie fluttered away.

The dark consumed her.

Katherine and Marie's Parents

Inside the faerie circle, a day later.

"We need to do something." Marianne MacDonald lowered to her knees in the faerie circle next to her husband. Her daughter was so close yet still beyond her touch, right where she'd fallen the day before. She called to the fae, "Marigold, please, we need you."

"I'm here." She shimmered into sight and kneeling, pressed her palm against Katherine's chest. "Wake, my child. 'Tis I, one of the fae."

Katherine stirred and coughed. Slowly, she opened her eyes then fumbled for the fae's hand. "Help me," she croaked.

"I have already promised to give you aid, although to survive your soul will need to be bound to another who already walks this Earth."

"Do something. Anything." Blood dribbled from Katherine's mouth.

"You will need to join your sister in the past. That is now your place. Look. She comes."

Marie snuck across the stony courtyard and passed under the arched entrance.

Marianne soaked in the sight of her firstborn child, as did her husband who gripped her hand.

"I'm here, Katherine." Marie slipped between two of the perimeter stones, knelt before the center stone and eyed Mary's amulet sitting upon it. "Where are you, sis?"

Katherine gurgled on blood and her eyes fluttered shut as she breathed her last.

"They can't see each other. Quickly, do something," Marianne urged the fae. "Katherine can't die."

Marigold closed her eyes and murmured, "I hereby bind Katherine MacLean's soul to the one man who should have always been hers. He lives in this time, her warrior protector. Send a piece of her inner light to him, so that he might guide and watch over her, throughout all time."

A bright light shimmered around Katherine's prone form and tendrils separated from her body and floated beyond the circle. As the fae swept her hands over Katherine, the wound on her neck closed and the blood drew away until not a drop remained. Marigold breathed into Katherine's mouth then stroked her cheek. "Wake, my child, but without fear. You shall no' remember what has happened here until you're ready."

Marianne held her breath.

Katherine gasped and dragged in precious air.

"'Tis done." Marigold nodded at Marianne. "In healing your daughter, her memories of the past day in this circle will be gone, but she will recall what is needed in time. 'Tis best that way."

Tears trickled down Marianne's cheeks. "Thank you."

"Come." Marigold drew her and Locky away. "We can no longer intervene or be seen."

"She needs to know we're here."

"Nay. For now, 'twill be too much for her to bear."

"Please, let Katherine come," Marie cried out to the fae as she thumped the short center stone. "I need her."

"I'm here." Katherine shook her groggy head and crawled closer to her sister. She swished her hand through Marie's form. "No. I can see you, but not touch you."

Marianne grasped her husband's hand. "They have to find each other, Locky."

"They will. Trust in the fae." He squeezed her hand in return.

"I can hear you, sis." Marie sagged forward. "I saw to Archie's wish. Lachlan MacLean lives and he's been taken by the king's men to Edinburgh as history has foretold. Our paternal line continues on. You and I will survive."

"Then come home to me. I'm between times."

"Marie!" Archie shouted her name as he raced down the trail, his white shirttails flying free behind him. The MacDonald warrior hit the edge of the circle, bounced off and slammed onto the ground. Stunned, he shook his head then staggered to his feet. "Hell, the veil's up."

"Take the amulet, sis." Katherine pleaded.

"Marie, is Katherine in there with you?" Archie shoved against the veil. "Dinnae go to her, no' yet. I need to hold you, one last time."

"Marie." Katherine clambered to her feet, her long blond hair whipping about her in the swirling breeze. "Every day since you disappeared into the past, I've returned and waited for you. I'm right here, and I've watched those ruins and wished for the castle to reappear. Pick up the amulet. It must be the only way you can get back to me."

"I don't want to leave him, but I'll never leave you." Marie wrapped shaky fingers around the amulet and slipped it over her head.

Katherine gasped and grabbed her sister as she appeared in full form before her. "Oh my goodness, you're back. I can finally touch you. You're real."

"We're together again." Marie mashed their wet cheeks

together.

"Archie!" Archie's brother raced down the trail, his warrior's sword at his side. "What's happened?"

"Marie's gone, John." Archie clutched the grass and ripped handfuls free. "She's gone."

"Then wish for Marie back, as you wished for her in the very beginning." John crouched beside Archie.

"This is what Marie wanted, to return to her sister. I willnae make her choose between her own kin and me." Archie seized his brother's arm. "I must give her up."

Katherine hugged Marie tight then looked into her eyes. "I can see Archie loves you."

"He has my heart." Marie peered at Archie, her gaze filled with such longing.

Katherine glanced between the warrior and her sister. "We should join them, Marie. There is nothing left for us in the future. Mum and Dad are gone. We have no other family." She swiped the talisman from around Marie's neck, clasped hands with her and wound the amulet around both their wrists. "Let's do this, but this time, we go together. You're not leaving me again."

"Are you sure?"

Marianne wrung her hands together. "Yes," she whispered to her daughters as she pressed them, "you must go together."

"It's been hard to live without our parents, so yes, I'm sure. Surely you don't want to lose another person you love too?" Katherine strode toward John and pressed her hand against the veil in front of him. "John, it's Katherine, Marie's sister. Tell Archie to make a wish, for both my sister and me."

"I hear you." The warrior rose and rested his hand over Katherine's. "Make a wish, Archie, for both of them. Katherine asks it of you."

"I'll try." Archie squeezed his eyes shut. "Guardians of Dunyvaig, I ask for a wish. For you to send me the woman who has stolen my heart and the one she holds closest to her. Bring them here, so we need never live apart again." He swept his hand through the air and Marie's amulet rose, breached the barrier and spun into his palm.

A wind rose and tunneled around Katherine and Marie, whipping their hair across their faces. Marie clutched hold of Katherine. "Don't let go of me, sis. If you do, you'll be in more trouble than it's worth."

"I'm holding on. Sisters, forever." Katherine peered back toward Marianne and Locky and smiled.

"Can she see us, Marigold?" Marianne touched her heart.

"Nay, and so too her memories of this past day in the circle are gone, but as kin, she senses your presence all the same. Look." The fae motioned toward the streaming tendrils of Katherine's essence which still swirled beyond the veil. They wisped around John and then absorbed into his body. "He is her warrior protector, the one always meant for her. He now holds a piece of her soul. The two are deeply bound."

The veil thinned and Katherine fell through the barrier and into John's arms.

"Katherine has made the right choice and lives." The fae smiled. "Now she must accept her fate and her new bond with her warrior. She cannae survive without him. To do so, will mean her ultimate death."

"Then that's a death I'll never allow." Marianne held firm to her words. She'd do whatever it took to ensure both her daughters' survival and that Katherine remembered all that had gone on within this circle. She couldn't be with them in life, but she would still safeguard their future happiness.

She'd watch over them as she always had.

Chapter 1

Dunyvaig Castle, MacDonald stronghold, 1590, two weeks following Katherine's arrival.

Katherine stood at her chamber window. Beyond the gates, the faerie circle remained quiet, bare of any breeze, and the amulet glinting in the moonlight upon the center stone where her sister had tossed it following their arrival into the past. Something within the circle called to her, demanding her return, just as her nightly dreams urged her to do the same.

She needed answers, and it was time. She grasped her burgundy skirts, strode out of her room and down the winding stairs. Hurrying, she bypassed the great hall, walked across the stony inner courtyard and under the arched entrance.

After taking a deep, fortifying breath, she stepped into the circle and stopped before the center stone. Slowly, reverently, she picked up the amulet and whispered, "Guardians of Dunyvaig, why have you brought me here?"

A breeze lifted her hair and made it tickle her face.

"My child," a voice breathed. "I've been waiting for you, to give you the guidance you seek."

"Am I real? Nightmares assail me and I see my death here

in this circle, a death I don't remember."

"Katherine, you no longer belong to the future, but here in the past. Wear the amulet. 'Tis yours to hold and will provide safe passage as you return to your MacLean kin."

"I'm to travel to the Isle of Mull?" Her sister was here and now wed to a MacDonald, her MacLean clan's greatest enemy. "Marie is away on her honeymoon. I can't leave her."

"You and your twin are two halves of one whole, the beginning and the end. You must complete what your sister has set in motion. Keep your warrior protector close. To bring peace, you must unite."

"My warrior protector?"

"Aye, the man who is ever watchful, the one who caught you as you fell into this time."

She slowly turned. High on the castle's battlements, John MacDonald stood with one hand resting on his sword hilt and the sea breeze plastering his blue tunic to his broad chest. "He's one of Angus MacDonald's captains. He can't travel with me to Mull and enter the enemy's territory."

"Aye, he can, if he does so for you. If that is what it will take for you to see the truth, then that is what must be." The fae's voice drifted on the wind, moving farther away. "You, my child, are of both clans, but there is more you arena aware of. There is magic all around you. Simply open your eyes if you wish to see it, then draw on the touch of fae blood you hold deep within you. You must accept your place in this time if you wish to survive."

"Hold on. I have fae blood?"

All was eerily still and no answer came. The fae had gone, and just as quickly as she'd come. And drat it. She was still without answers. Were her nightmares real?

Hands shaking, she lifted the talisman's silver chain over her head and pressed the amulet against her heart. She had a mission, and the fae's words reverberated through her mind. *Keep your warrior protector close. To bring peace, you must unite.* Bringing some peace between the clans was what she longed for. A strange sense of rightness stole over her. As Marie had completed her mission and saved their paternal ancestor, so too, she'd complete hers. She wouldn't let the fae down.

She trod out of the circle and climbed the stairs to the battlements, toward the one man who never veered far from her side.

Ahead, John pushed away from the thick stone crenellation and arms crossed, observed her. "What were you doing in the circle?"

"Seeking advice." Only John, Archie and Mary knew the truth of how she and Marie had come to travel from the future here to the past. "I spoke to one of the fae."

"You must take care. Even as the little folk guard Dunyvaig, they also tinker and play."

She palmed the amulet at her neck. It's silver surface glimmered in the moonlight.

"Tell me why you hold Mary's talisman. 'Twas left in the circle for a reason." With one finger under her chin, John lifted her gaze to his. "You can always speak to me."

"I know." Warmth from his gentle touch rolled through her. "The fae told me this amulet is now mine to hold and will provide safe passage as I return to my MacLean kin."

"You were asked to travel to Duart Castle on the Isle of Mull?"

"Yes. I've been given a mission."

"Nay, I'll never allow you to step one foot on MacLean territory, mission or no'." He pressed her against the stone wall at her back, enclosing her fully in his heat. "The danger is too great. Tell me exactly what the fae said."

"That Marie and I are two halves of one whole, the beginning and the end. I'm to complete what my sister has set in motion. She also said to keep my warrior protector close. To bring peace, we must unite." She pushed against him but he budged not an inch. "John, don't go getting all muscly-man on me."

"Shh, take care with your strange words. Voices can travel along the battlements and the other guards are close." He eased one hand under her shoulders and the other behind her head, protecting her from the rough stone. "While Archie is away, you're my responsibility. Traveling to Mull willnae happen on my watch. They're the enemy."

"Your enemy, not mine. I'm a MacLean, in case you forgot." She wriggled her trapped hands free from between them and sighed. "The Chief of MacLean will father my paternal line, just as Mary MacDonald will give birth to my maternal one. I may be living in the past, but in truth, I've yet to be born. Even Mary wishes for peace between the clans."

"Of which you've assured me does no' happen for many years. If you attempt to bring about peace, then you'd be changing the future, something you and Marie are adamant against doing. Now enough of this talk of traveling to Mull. 'Tis late and you need your rest." He tucked her under his shoulder and led her toward the stairs.

"The fae wouldn't have asked me to travel to Duart Castle if I wasn't supposed to."

"Mayhap what the fae said is no' all you believe. Consider their words well." He called out to the guardsman in the gatehouse, "Lower the portcullis. Secure the keep for the night."

The portcullis within the stone-arched entrance lowered, its clunky chains reverberating throughout the keep.

"I'm twenty-one, John. You can't demand I go to bed just because that suits you."

"I can and I did."

He was so frustrating.

"You also don't need to watch over me as intensely as you do." In the past fortnight, she'd barely slept, her dreams always swirling with darkness and death. Her cries had woken John that first night and ever since, he'd slept in her room, watching over her. "I'm not a child."

"I'm well aware." He opened the door and motioned her into the great hall.

"I spoke to the fae about my nightmares."

"You did?" He lifted one eyebrow. "And…"

"She said I no longer belonged to the future, but here in the past. Not much of an answer."

"Well, I agree you belong here, although I wish you'd speak to me of what awakens you at night."

"I'm sorry." She shook her head. "Perhaps it's my grief manifesting. I'm not sure. All I know is I miss them."

"Your parents?"

"Yes." Losing her mother to cancer a few short months ago had near broken her heart, as it had her sister's, particularly when it had come so close on the heels of their father's passing the year before. "Don't you miss your parents?"

His father had died on the battlefield the year he'd turned eighteen, and his mother on the day she'd given birth to him and Archie. How awful. He'd never even gotten to know his own mother.

"I think of them constantly. 'Tis best to allow only the good memories to surface." He guided her upstairs to the third floor, ushered her into her chamber and shut the door. Crouched before the hearth, he tore strips of bark from a log and brought a flame to life striking flint with his dagger. A fire soon blazed and spread its heat through the room. Hands dusted, he rose and crossed to the navy corner padded chair he'd slept in these past two weeks and plumped the pillow. With a deep sigh, he removed his sword belt, set it against the side of the chair then tucked a loose blue shirttail back into his black leather pants.

"I wish the nightmares would stop. I hate that I'm keeping you from your bed."

"Until they cease, I'll remain at your side. Do you need me

to unlace your gown?"

"Yes, please." She turned her back and he stepped in behind her. Holding the burgundy velvet bodice to her chest, she smiled over her shoulder at him. "In the future, one doesn't need this kind of help when undressing."

"Do you miss your men's trews?" A teasing glint lit his eyes as he scooped her hair and slid it to one side.

"They're called jeans, and in the twenty-first century, men and women both wear them, and yes, I do miss them." She'd fallen through the veil in her favorite skinny jeans and quite shocked John when she'd removed her tartan red and blue woolen coat to uncover them. "It's amazing to see how proficient you're getting at this task, although sleeping in my chamber must be giving your single status a knock."

"Single status? Another interesting term of yours." Chuckling, his breath puffed warmly against her back as he exposed her skin. "All here are aware of your nightmares and that I must maintain a vigil at your bedside. Your good name remains intact."

"My good name doesn't worry me."

"It should." A frown furrowed his brow.

"Well, I didn't mean it quite like that. It's just I'm here in the past and I have to be so careful. I can't take the risk of changing anyone's future. That means I'm keeping my own single status."

"Your sister happily changed Archie's future by agreeing to be his wife."

"Archie had already decreed he'd never join with another, and well before Marie had ever arrived. She changed nothing."

"You wish to live your life without ever knowing love?" He loosened the last lacing.

"No, but I'm out of choices." Bodice scrunched in her hands, she faced him. "Do you wish to marry one day?"

"Aye, I wish to wed, to find a wife who'll give me strong

sons and feisty daughters."

"Have you ever courted a woman?" She toed off her silk slippers, nabbed her nightrail from her trunk and eased behind the silk dressing screen hand painted with a beautiful field of heather.

"Nay, and usually a man has to prove what he can offer when considering marriage, either by the strength of his sword arm, or by the lands he owns."

"Do you have any land?" He certainly had a strong sword arm and she'd admired his fighting form often as he'd trained with his men. The man had muscles on top of muscles.

"A small parcel on Argyll adjacent to my brother's. 'Twas land we received upon our father's death. 'Tis no' much, but there is a castle, even as rundown as it is."

"Then why are you here and not there?" She shimmied out of her gown, tossed it over the top of the screen and donned her white cotton shift.

"The Isle of Islay is the land of my kin, and I'm still earning enough coin to effect adequate repairs on the castle. 'Twill be a beauty one day, solid and strong."

"I'd love to see your land."

"If you wish it, I will gladly take you. 'Tis but a short sail, except that any trip there would have to wait until the current threat from the MacLean clan eases."

She walked out from behind the screen.

Lathering soap, James stood before the basin on the side table, his leather pants molding his tight butt and providing a delectable sight. He smeared bubbles along his jaw as he bent to the task.

Smiling, she crossed and lifted his shoulder-length brown locks wisped with blond. "My mother used to hold my father's hair whenever he shaved. It saved getting suds in his hair. I'm not sure why, but he preferred the old hand razor over an electric shaver."

"What's an electric shaver?" His golden gaze met hers in the looking glass propped before him.

"It's a device which plugs into a power source and when turned on, has sharp metal rotating heads that slice the stubble off at the root. No soap and blade is necessary."

"Is this the power source you called elec-tri-city?" He twisted his tongue around the foreign word she'd mentioned a few nights ago when she'd explained how energy was contained and dispersed, how electricity brought heat and light into a room and how it powered devices big and small. She'd boggled his mind when she'd spoken of email, letters that could be sent with the press of one button to anyone in the world.

"That's right."

"Do you miss the conveniences of your time? Many sound miraculous." He slid his dagger from ear to chin in one smooth move.

"Not yet, but I'm sure I will." She leaned into his back and covered his hand holding the blade. "Can I try that?"

He stopped, one brow raised. "You wish to shave me?"

"I saw a maid doing so for one of the warriors yesterday in the great hall. Is it not the right thing to ask?"

"The warrior you're speaking of is George. Three weeks past, he was hit by an arrow when Lachlan MacLean attacked Mary and Marie's party as they returned to Dunyvaig from the village of Ardbeg. The arrow embedded deep into his side and he cannae yet lift his arm. The maid shaves him so he willnae tear his stitches."

"Oh, I didn't realize."

He faced her, rested his backside on the table and extended his dagger toward her. "Shave me. I dinnae have an issue with it."

"Are you sure?"

"Aye, but take it slow." He pressed his dirk into her hands, cupped her hips and held her steady between his spread legs.

"I promise I'll do a good job." Turning his cheek with one finger, she held the blade nice and close to his skin and ran it in a smooth line down. "I'm also a quick learner, and if I make a mistake, I'll see it."

"My blood's red by the way." He squeezed her hips.

"So is mine." Grinning, she drew the dagger along the next portion under his chin and down his throat. "Goodness. It's like slicing through butter. I thought your stubble would be rougher to cut."

"I keep my dagger fastidiously sharp. Is that fire providing enough light?" His gaze darted toward it.

"Oh, no, you don't. I wouldn't move if I were you." She ran the blade right under his nose. "You wouldn't want me to nick this smart mouth of yours."

"I—"

"Don't speak either." She tapped his jaw shut and giggled. "This is so much fun. I never thought I'd ever get one-up on you." She shaved the bristles around his lips, not missing even one blade. "Mmm, that's smooth."

"Aye, there shall be no more whisker burn for the lasses after you're done."

"Then you can tell them to thank me." She slid the blade along the last stretch of his neck then dabbed his skin dry with the cloth. "Take a look in the glass. What do you think?"

He observed his reflection, patted his jawline and traced around his lips. "You've done a better job than I ever could have."

"Do you mind if I use your dagger to shave as well?" She wiped his blade clean on the cloth.

"Nay." His smile died away. "You're no' to take a blade to your soft skin."

"But my legs are itchy. I've never let them get so hairy."

"I said nay." He held out his hand for his dagger. "Women do no' shave their legs."

"They shave an awful lot more than that in my time." She passed it back, trod to her navy canopied bed and clambered under the covers. "I'll ask Mary for a blade in the morning."

"And I'll make sure she does no' give you one." He settled in his armchair, the pillow tucked behind his head.

"Then I'll pinch one from one of the warrior's when they're not watching."

"I'd like to see you try." He rolled his neck, scrunched his face then rubbed his nape as if in pain.

"John." She patted the space next to her and sighed. "Come and sleep beside me. I can't stand to see you so cramped and this bed is plenty big enough for both of us."

"Are you certain?"

"Yes, and the fact you're not saying no proves just how much you need to rest somewhere more comfortable than that chair. Please, it'll ease some of my guilt. It's my fault you feel indebted to remain."

"Aye, a fortnight in this chair has been long enough." He walked to the door, slid the bolt home then grabbed his pillow and ambled toward her. After sliding in under the covers, he stared at the wooden paneled ceiling above, a thoughtful look on his face. "I shouldnae ask, but where else does a woman shave? You've completely baffled me."

"I'll tell you, but only if you spill a secret about yourself as well." She snuggled into his side. The man exuded heat from every pore and the bed was cold. She may as well take advantage of the fact he could warm her quicker than anything else.

"Aye, that I can do." He wrapped one arm around her waist as he rolled onto his side and faced her. "Ladies first."

"Well, I've always preferred to remain bare below. I've waxed for years and I like feeling smooth, very smooth."

"Surely you cannae mean you wax your—" His gaze traveled down her body and he groaned.

"Yes, I wax down there."

"Oh hell. Clearly I shouldnae have asked." His cheeks flushed and she smiled.

"Waxing doesn't hurt, and I'm used to it although these days the candle wax I'm using takes a little more care and preparation compared to the modern day formula. Now it's your turn. Tell me your deepest, darkest secret."

"My secret isnae as personal as yours, but when I was a lad, I set out on an adventure. As I scaled Islay's cliffs, I discovered a hidden shaft covered by thick bushes."

"Oh, I love exploring. What did you find?"

"This particular shaft led to a sacred underground cavern. Except I couldnae wriggle through the last few feet to the interior, so instead I backed out and scoured the forest beyond the cliffs for another way in. That's when I discovered a tunnel winding deep into the earth. It came out afore a heavenly pool of crystal clear hot water."

"And you've never spoken of this to another?" She tucked a lock of his hair that had flopped forward, back behind his ear.

"I've no' told a soul, no' even Archie. This place is mine alone."

"Where is it, exactly?" There were cliffs all over Islay. It could be anywhere. "I'll never tell another soul either. I promise."

"'Tis no' far from here."

"Will you show me?" *Please say yes.*

"That might require us making another bargain." He picked up the amulet at her neck, closed his fingers around it and gently tugged her closer. "What do you wish to offer up for such a valuable piece of information?"

"The ultimate gift." She touched her nose to his and grinned. "I promise not to argue with you for one entire day."

Hmm, let him try not to take that bait.

* * * *

John chuckled as mischief danced in Katherine's big blue

eyes. She knew just how to tempt and entice him as no other woman ever had. "That is one tempting offer, little imp."

"I do try."

"I will need to think on it." He slid his fingers through her long white-blond hair glimmering gold in the firelight. "But mayhap from that chair. Being in the same bed as you is addling my senses."

"Nothing addles you." She traced the indent in his chin then kissed the spot. "Please, I'd love to see your sacred cavern."

"Mayhap if you spoke of your nightmares and shared the burden, I might consider that a justifiable bargain." He stroked down her sides and over her hips. "They haunt you and I cannae stand it."

"You strike a hard bargain." She breathed deep and slowly nodded. "All right. In my nightmares I see my death."

"What?" Surely she jested, only from the firm expression on her face, she didn't.

"When I'm asleep, I keep reliving the moment before I arrived, while I was stuck between times inside the faerie circle. I see myself bleeding from a wound on my neck." She nibbled on her lower lip and he rubbed his thumb along the reddened mark.

"Continue. I wish to hear it all."

"My dreams feel more like returning memories."

"You came through the veil with no wounds."

"Yes, which makes my dreams all the more strange." She trailed a finger down his neck and into the deep V of his tunic. "Do you recall Marie's neck wound?"

"Aye. When Archie took his blade to Lachlan during the battle at the Rhinns, Marie cried out and clasped her neck as a wound suddenly opened out of nowhere. Archie held his hand against MacLean, then bound hers and Lachlan's wounds. She bled because her paternal ancestor did."

"In my dreams, I suffered the same injury as Marie, in the

exact same spot."

"Archie didnae take MacLean's life. He bound her wound and she survived."

"There was so much blood, and I had no one there to stem the flow like Marie did."

"Nay, I dinnae believe it. You're alive and have no' perished." He pulled her closer, held her tight.

"I also dream of my parents. They were there with me in the circle and I have no idea how that could've happened, not when—" Tears pooled in her eyes. "I fought for each breath I could until one of the fae shimmered into sight and pressed again my chest. The heat of her touch moved through my body and everything felt so peaceful."

"I was there when you came through the veil." He aligned every inch of their bodies. "You were well and truly alive with no' a drop of blood on you."

"Yes, but I think the fae must have removed it. The next thing I remember is coming to and hearing Marie call my name. Then you and Archie arrived." She sniffed. "I know it all seems strange, but the moment you and I touched, I felt like I'd just come home, as if I was whole again."

"You are home when you're with me." Rubbing his cheek against hers, he gave into the deep need within him to draw her even closer. He rolled her onto her back and looked deep into her shimmering blue eyes. "Katherine, may I kiss you?"

Her breath hitched and her pupils darkened. "There's something about you that calls to me, but kissing really should be off the table."

"That's no' the answer I seek."

"If there's one thing I've learnt, history must remain on course." She raised a brow. "I can't change the path you're supposed to travel, and kissing me isn't part of that path."

"One kiss willnae change my future."

"You're also a temptation I need to resist."

"And you're a temptation I have no intention of resisting." He brushed his mouth over hers, so gently, so softly, then as she softened underneath him, he urged her lips farther apart and delved deeper into the delicious recesses of her mouth. Desire swarmed his senses and he feasted, kissing her as he'd secretly longed to since the moment they'd met.

"Oh my goodness, are we truly kissing?" She melted against him, her breath whispering softly across his tongue in a teasing caress he wanted more of.

"Aye, and I need another." He kissed her again, indulging and welcoming the raw intimacy he hadn't a chance of halting.

"You make me feel so alive, John." She tugged his shirttails free and slipped her hands underneath his tunic. Palms warm against his flesh, she stroked along his sides and over his lower back. "Tonight, the fae also told me there was magic all around me, and to draw on the touch of fae in my blood."

"You have fae in your blood?" He lifted up and stared into her eyes.

"Not that I've ever known. Neither of my parents certainly ever mentioned a thing." She pressed her breasts against his chest, kissed along his jaw and nibbled his ear. "You taste so good. Even though I shouldn't, I like kissing you."

"If you are part fae then that would explain how you so easily scatter my thoughts." He rubbed his hips against hers and his cock stiffened and pushed into her belly. "Aye, and far too much." He blew out a long breath and flopped onto his back. "My apologies. I've let things go too far."

"Don't be sorry."

"'Tis time for us to sleep." He fisted his hands so as not to reach for her again. "Rest, Katherine. I'll watch over you throughout the night."

"I know you will." She closed her eyes and as her breathing evened out, she fell asleep.

He too allowed sleep to take him.

Highlander Heat

Highlander's Castle, Book One
Highlander's Magic, Book Two
Highlander's Charm, Book Three
Highlander's Guardian, Book Four
Highlander's Faerie, Book Five
Highlander's Champion, Book Six

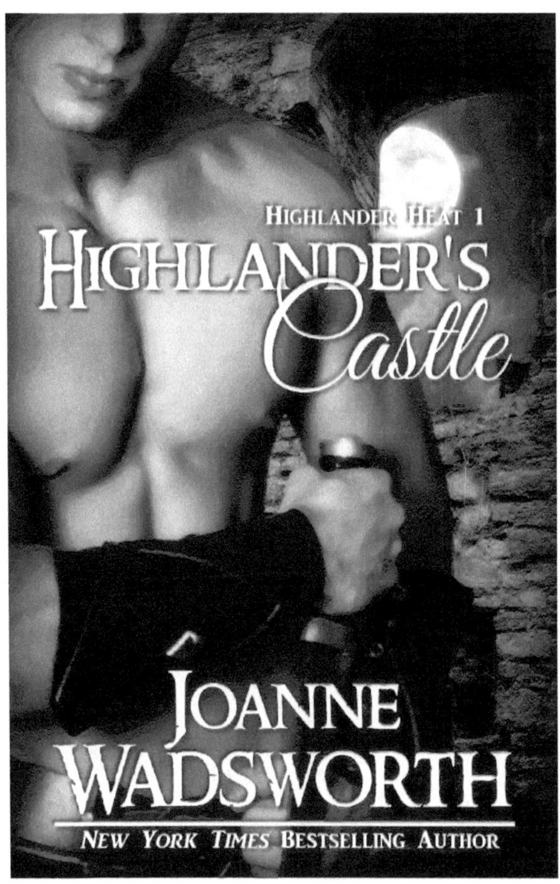

The Matheson Brothers

Highlander's Desire, Book One
Highlander's Passion, Book Two
Highlander's Seduction, Book Three

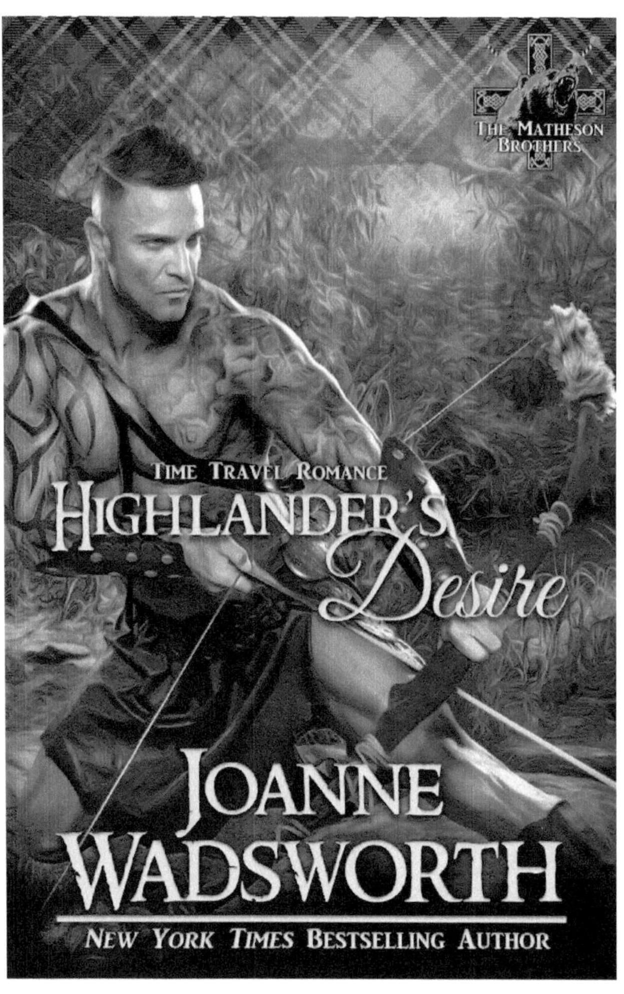

The Matheson Brothers Continued

Highlander's Kiss, Book Four
Highlander's Heart, Book Five
Highlander's Sword, Book Six

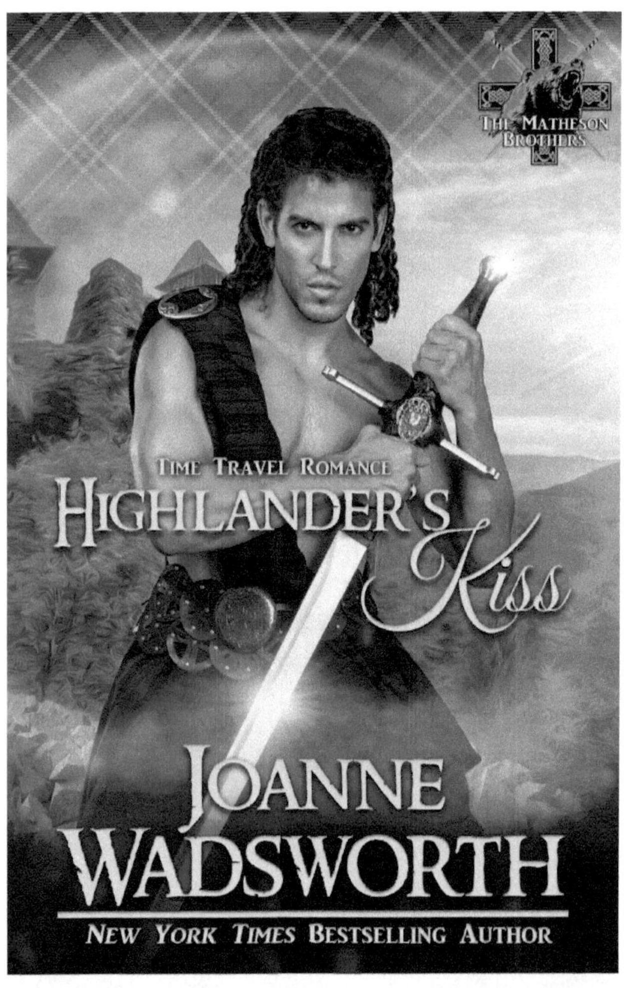

The Matheson Brothers Continued

Highlander's Bride, Book Seven
Highlander's Caress, Book Eight
Highlander's Touch, Book Nine

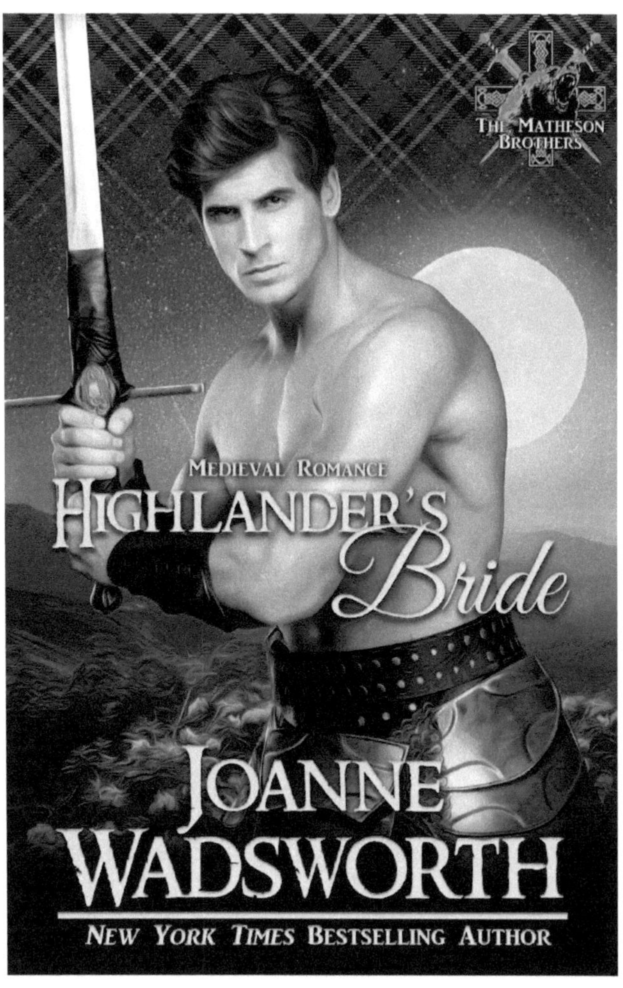

The Matheson Brothers Continued

Highlander's Shifter, Book Ten
Highlander's Claim, Book Eleven
Highlander's Courage, Book Twelve
Highlander's Mermaid, Book Thirteen

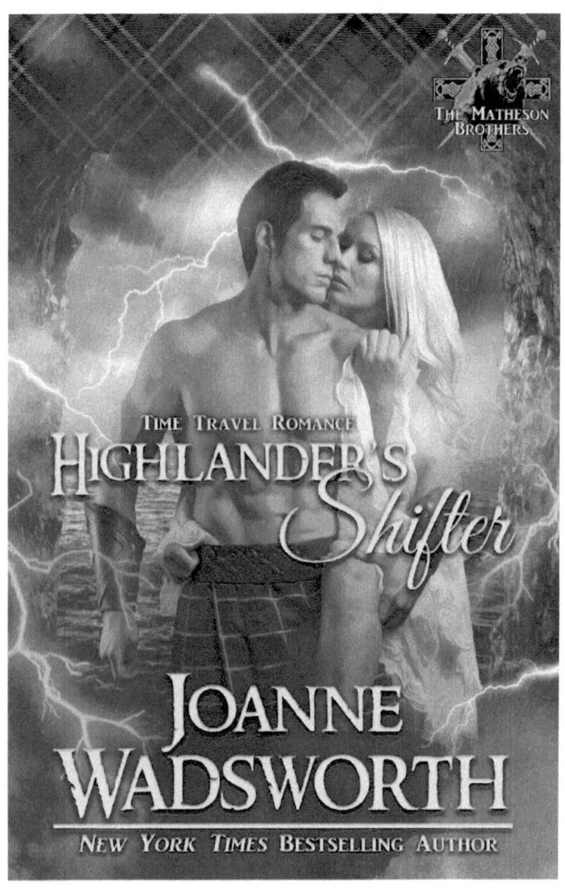

Princesses of Myth

JOANNE WADSWORTH

Billionaire Bodyguards

Billionaire Bodyguard Attraction, Book One
Billionaire Bodyguard Boss, Book Two
Billionaire Bodyguard Fling, Book Three

JOANNE WADSWORTH

Joanne Wadsworth is a *New York Times* and *USA Today* Bestselling Author who adores getting lost in the world of romance, no matter what era in time that might be. Hot alpha Highlanders hound her, demanding their stories are told and she's devoted to ensuring they meet their match, whether that be with a feisty lass from the present or far in the past.

Living on a tiny island at the bottom of the world, she calls New Zealand home. Big-dreamer, hoarder of chocolate, and addicted to juicy watermelons since the age of five, she chases after her four energetic children and has her own hunky hubby on the side.

So come and join in all the fun, because this kiwi girl promises to give you her "Hot-Highlander" oath, to bring you a heart-pounding, sexy adventure from the moment you turn the first page. This is where romance meets fantasy and adventure…

To learn more about Joanne and her works, visit
http://www.joannewadsworth.com